George Henry Walser

Poems of Leisure

George Henry Walser

Poems of Leisure

ISBN/EAN: 9783337408190

Printed in Europe, USA, Canada, Australia, Japan

Cover: Foto ©Andreas Hilbeck / pixelio.de

More available books at **www.hansebooks.com**

Poems of Leisure.

—BY—

G. H. WALSER.

Lamar, Missouri.
South-West Missourian Print.
1890.

PREFACE.

Mine has been a busy life, devoted to the first duty of providing for my family and the winters of old age. Through industry, I am now able to think that I have enough to keep the wolf from the door of myself and wife, (my family, now), provided we act with prudence and economy. All persons at the age of fifty should have that; to have less is a mistake, to have more is a sin.

In arranging my affairs for retiring from active business, I have exhumed from my old portfolio, the musings of Leisure Hours, covering the period of many years, which I wish to preserve for the pleasure they afforded me in their production. To do that, I have concluded to reproduce them in book form.

But few of the ensuing poems have ever been published, and, I am sure the public does not know me as a rhymester, much less as a poet, the honor of which I can scarcely hope of receiving. Many can write rhymes; but few can write poetry. Poetry consists in clothing elevating thoughts in chaste and rhythmic language. If I have succeeded in doing that, I will feel that the presentation of this volume is not presumptuous. If I have failed, in the estimation of the public, my feelings of pride will be wounded to some degree. Yet, with all that, I will have enough left for our family.

I have written as subjects have presented themselves to me: and endeavored to picture them on paper as they impressed themselves on my mind, without reference to my individual convictions. There will be found, woven in these poems, Atheistic, Spiritualistic and Christian thoughts. They were written for their beauty and suggestive thoughts. I find beauty, love, sublimity and usefulness all around me and among every people, sect and denomination. The great differences are in thoughts, not in facts.

It affords me exquisite pleasure to get in rapport with the highest conceptions of the good and becoming, wherever they may be found. Such has been my aim in the production of this book.

With my best wishes for all and malice for none, I send this adventurer forth.

G. H. Walser.

Liberal, Missouri.

Poems of Leisure.

FAREWELL TO THE BAR.

Farewell to the bar! farewell to the cases!
Farewell to the rolls my memory embraces!
I leave thee forever, with many regrets,
And joys behind none ever forgets.

Around thee there cluster the fondest of ties,
Successes with laughter, defeats with their sighs:
And all rounding up, with battles completed,
With someone as victor, someone defeated.

It is not the battle that soldiers reflect.
The sword that is used is the keen intellect:
And the scars that leave their red traces behind,
Are made by the keen rapier of the mind.

The fields o' thy prowess have infinite changes,
Thy scope is the bounds where intellect ranges:
With all the perfections, at every flaw,
The barrister stands in the bloom of the law.

In all enterprises that mankind attends,
Of whatever nature, the law comprehends,
Be them the most humble or abject in tone,
The law is as vigil as ruling a throne.

Man's rights were proscribed by the whims of the rex,
In the days of whilom, but now it is lex
That spreads its arm over all, ample and strong,
And a remedy gives for each human wrong.

The farm and the workshop, the forge and the mill,
Whatever of labour, of science, or skill,
Of trade e'en small: or, great enterprises,
For pleasure, or profit, the law supervises.

It plods with the cartman and flies with the train.
It sports with the shallop and plows the broad main.
It ticks with the telegraph and speaks with the pen,
And the press that paints greatness on very small men.

'Tis the guide of the judge, demure and sedate,
And it reigns supreme in the councils of state,
And rules with the fiat of one in command,
Ev'ry action of man, on sea, or on land.

It guards ev'ry right and curbs ev'ry wrong,
Meets even justice to the weak and the strong,
Demolishes rank and pretense everywhere,
And makes ev'ry man ev'ry other man's peer.

The why of this all is of easy discerning,
The law is the acme of reason and learning;
And gives each his meed, without favor or fear,
When a lawyer is placed at the helm to steer.

Farewell to the bar and statute provisions!
Farewell to the bench and its crispy decisions!
Farewell to keen gybes and forensic foolings,
And gauling rebukes by hot-headed rulings!

Farewell to the noblest of noble professions!
Farewell to praecipes and declarations,
To pleas, replies, rejoinders and rebutters,
Likewise surrejoinders and surrebutters!

Demurrers and motions *ad infinitude*,
Holes in the practice, through which scoundrels elude
The vigils of Astrea, who sees with awe,
Rogues honorable made by evading the law.

And all of the phases and technical terms,
At which justice recoils and roguery yearns,
I leave to attorneys more wily than I,
Whose conscience are caught by the size of the fee.

The forum, where logic and sophistry blend
To make a dull jury a point comprehend,
Where Justice is baffled and glories are won,
And eloquence killed by the point of a pun.

Farewell to the members who honor the bar!
The force of your worth is felt everywhere,
The crown of your glory can ev'ryone see,
And surely you need no encomium from me.

Genial of mind and of manners polite,
Acute of discernment and sticklers for right,
And all the prime virtues bow at your command,

You rule all the world with your heart in your hand.

Your brain is the fountain of every field
To the bearing of which, all others must yield;
In great undertakings your council is sought,
At the fount of your mind all satiate draught.

Trusts of all kinds are reposed to your keeping.
Secrets of hearts you are never repeating.
Loads that are borne on the face of a breath
Are given to you in the presence of death.

Wealth, favors and fortunes are placed in your care.
Responsible trusts that no others can bear,
With the guarantee only from you in return.
The bar has an honor no power can turn.

In contests for right are ever aggressive.
In proper reforms are always progressive;
You never complain that the world goes too fast.
Or bridle the future with th' tail of the past.

Yes! in turning away my lingering mind
Goes back to the scenes it is leaving behind;
With many regrets, sad, that Time will renew,
With my heart entombed in this long, last adieu.

THE CASCADE.

I gazed on the breaks of a cascade
    And felt an emotion sublime,
As I saw it leap down a great facade,
    That looked like the brother of Time.
The scaur that reached high above us
    Held back the impress of a tarn,
Whose bosom supported the lotos,
    Whose verge wore trousseau of fern.

I gazed on the waters down leaping,
    And the rock-rooted trees overhead,
Whose moan in the high winds were keeping
    In tune with the cataract mad.
I looked, and above the clear fountain,
    Above the tall trees bending o'er,
And saw in the background a mountain
    That kissed the cerulean shore.

I turned with the cataract's roar
And saw it rush on to the plain,
Which caught its mad plunge from the scaur
And bore it away to the main.
And as it rolled on to the ocean,
Its fret and its gnarl passed away
And sank to a gentler motion,
A grave and sublimer display.

It moved with a harmonic union,
With a grandeur and beauty complete.
To join in fraternal communion
The far reaching swell of the deep;
Whose face leads away to the distance
Where the sky and the ocean meet;
Where the waves with becoming obeisance
Kiss Heaven's cerulean feet.

And I thought of the drifting of Youth;
Of his source next to Heaven complete.
Of his eschewing the mandates of truth
And his plunge o'er the precipice steep:
And then of the long rolling years,
Of moil and regrets of the past,
Of his sorrows that burn into tears:
His reaching for Heaven at last.

HESTER AND PHILO—A TRANCE.

—:—

PREFACE.

The facts forming the basis of the following narrative were partly given to me by a person who experienced the journey to the great abyss of chaos while he was in a trance.

Many good people believe in the duality of man, and that the spirit, while in a trans-condition, does go on vast journeys, and in some instances it retains in the mind impressions of the places and scenes it visited.

Some of the narrative is imaginative and some drawn from the Buddhistic religion and some from the Philosophy of Spiritualism.

The production of the narrative has given me much pleasurable speculation, and if its perusal inspires a kindred pleasure, my work will not have been in vain.

CANTO I.

I.

Who hath not felt the eyes of young love pierce
His inner self, like fiery darts of pleasure?
　　Who hath not felt his yearning breast aflame
At a word; and a sweet smile, like a fierce
Dagger, course his ev'ry nerve with the measure
　　Of ecstatic joy, again and again?

II.

Hester's large, brown eyes were the counterpart
Of Heaven.　All of earth was in her smile;
　　All of bliss was in her voice.　Her presence
Brought that electric glow that only a heart,
A captive, lead by love, can feel.　The while
　　I a boy, she a girl, brought these pleasance.

III.

I never spoke of love to her; yet, there
Is a language too refined for the tongue,
　　Too expressive far for thought words to mean.
The language of the eye speaks its volumes,
Heaven wills it, the heart drinks it.　Wrung
　　From the soul is that ecstatic heart-beam.

IV.

In our school days, the apple did not well
Impart its flavor, did Hester have not
　　One.　The class was dull, were we not conning

Side by side, our books.   I never could tell
    Why: but all seemed wrong, had Hester forgot,
    And tardy made the hour of her coming.

v.

At play, some how, we would be on the same
    Side.   The babbling brooklet did not its sweet
        Music enchant the ear, if one alone
Was there.   Oft Hester, in voice mild, would name
    Where flowers sweet were grown.   A cool retreat
        Was loved by both; its beauties both would own.

vi.

Time, its weary length rolled on.   Hester grew
    To be a woman, I a man.   The way
        To school was left, its wilders to confer
On others.   We parted.   I never knew.
    And yet I knew, though never heard her say,
        She loved.   Never my tongue confessed to her.

vii.

Sad were the lonely, lonely years that hung
    Like a pall of death upon me.   Sought I
        Relief in the solitudes of life.   Buried
Oft in solemn meditations, I sung
    Of the weird and lonesome.   In the deep sky,
        Among the floating orbs my mind tarried.

viii.

I would look upon the nebulosity
    In space and ride in my mind, on cloud flows,
        From whose ocean face of ether, deep-waved.
I would see Hester, whose vivacity
    Of love life, kept in my bosom the rose
        Flush of heaven wherein my soul was graved.

ix.

Would I curse my dull tongue often, and blame
    The unquenched fire of my sad and lonely heart
        For it, the store of words would not avail
Me, when her presence, so beloved, came
    In view: and I, quite bewildered, the part
        Could but play, of a tongue-tied youth, and fail.

x.

Sore of heart: and, by unrequited love.

Subdued in spirit, in a quiet shade
 I lay myself adown, careworn and weak,
Perhaps it was to die. I cared not. Above
Hung the mysteries of the deep. I made
An effort to rise, but could not, or speak.

XI.

I felt a wave like sleep on me falling—
 More than sleep it seemed, my nerves felt benumbed.
 And, segregating, my flesh seemed from my-
Self. My senses were alive, but calling (1)
 To my inner self, by a deep low-hummed
 Voice, stirred me. It seemed afar, yet close by.

XII.

The voice pulled me from myself. As I went
 Behind I cast a furtive glance and saw
 My former form, upon the deep green sward,
Pale and death-like, lying. A smile had spent
 Its force upon my face, wan and weird. How
 It was, I could not tell, or speak a word.

XIII.

As upon silken pinions I arose,
 Like with the grace of a zephyr dancing
 On the face of a morning sunbeam clear
And mild. Away I floated to the close
 Of another scene; to me enhancing
 Rich thoughts of a grander and brighter sphere.

XIV.

O'er my dim eyes a translucent wave came.
 I saw, or seem'd to see, what never I
 Beheld before; cities, mountains and streams
Beneath me pass. The while, I heard a strain
 Through the diapason of nature ply
 Its chords, melodious, like orphean dreams.

XV.

On rushing, I seem'd to go, outstretching
 Space whose capacious vastness seem'd subdu'd.
 My care was now my left friends, whose surprise
Unbounded, would be to learn o' my breaching
 The mysteries of Psyche and deep solitude,
 Where dead men in formless forms arise.

XVI.

But I rush'd on unconscious of the where,
  Or how. Lakes, oceans and continents pass'd
    And I, as a lost bird, pinion'd for flight
Eternal, onward sped. Voiced from San Poo fair,
  I bent my course; and, on a recluse cast
    My eye in Himalaya's topmost height.

XVII.

There, in the deep voice of solitude (2)
  Adepts of the black art abide in caves,
    And, from their dark, sepulchral homes emerge,
To greet a stranger with th' solicitude
  Of interested inquiry, which saves
    One the trouble of an acquaintance to urge.

XVIII.

Among them, I was a timorous man,
  Scarce knowing, a tongue I had, or, could speak
    My cause. But, ere my senses mustered up
Fair courage, the one, weirdest of the clan
  Breathed on my ear, in accents low and weak,
    That I should go with him where Time was not.

XIX.

Surprised and bewilder'd at what I heard,
  A feeling of doubt, father of distrust,
    Enwoof'd my mind. As I fathomed his speech
I felt it untrue, although not a word
  Parted my lips, but I felt that it must
    A vagary be he desired to reach.

XX.

I see from your mind, my words you distrust?
  Procleus, in voice, most musical said:
    "Without further doubting, give me your
Hand and then we'll away to the uttermost
  Bound of the universe, beyond the spread
    Of day, where the deep, fathomless shore

XXI.

Of darkness, was born; there will be no earth:
  The sun will go out and the constellation
    Of bright stars and all those jeweled lists
Of night will fade away and give birth,
  Again, to Chaos, whose habitation (3)
    Is the catalysis of cosmic mists.

XXII.

We arose. The air seemed tongued and did speak
In strains of eloquence, heard not before.
It seemed to stir my blood and move my
Soul by impressions unspeakable. Weak,
Too weak is mind to hold, or e'en explore
In thought, the mysteries chaotic that lie

XXIII.

Anterior to the all great world life
Of matter. We are lost, lost in mind grasp,
At the immensity of that winding
Sheet that threw its sable folds of night, rife
With eternal blackness, across the gaps
Of Chaos, which lies beyond our finding.

XXIV.

The astral knows no bounds. Attenuate (4)
We were and fledged for flight beyond the lists
Of world life, on wings of thought. A mind
We had to soar away and not to wait
Longer for the starting; for, much I wist
To test our might to leave the world behind.

XXV.

Our motors were our wills, for each were form'd (5)
With might to think and fly where we would—
Embodied mind, we were. With ease could fly
To the uttermost and then could rebound
In flight like lightning's flash through solitude.
Such was our procinct that the bending sky

XXVI.

Held no control of us. Its vaults gave way;
Its azure fled on either side, as up
Its vastitudes we went, as borne on
The pinions of electric thought. Away
Bounding, out vying time. With one grand swoop
We left the world behind; yet, tarried long

XXVII.

That we might well th' vastness investigate,
Of the scenes around us. All, a wonder
Was to us. All, one great mystery seem'd.—
Ourselves, a mystery. To demonstrate
The great procinct of man, we wish to ponder
And as we thought, and thought, perhaps we dreamed.

XXVIII.

That we might learn the truthful histories
   Of spheres and worlds, slowly on wings,
      Like seraphs, for observation we rose;
Sly casting lingering looks on mysteries
   Left behind, upon the earth, which springs
      New and pleasing beauties as on she goes.

XXIX.

Waiting, waiting away on the bosom
   Of ether, until our world on kindred
      Wing, the epitome of beauty seem'd.
We saw the golden streamlet of fulsome
   Sun-rays setting aglow the on-wing-word
      World with radiant strains as they gleamed.

XXX.

As we looked again, we saw up creeping
   The purple morn, above the orient,
      As evening spread upon the western verge,
A smile between light and darkness keeping
   Pace, while laughing day his out-spread wings blent
      The two extremes, and, night became the targe.

XXXI.

There Old Ocean, dress'd in marine blue, lay
   Beneath us, bearing her face to catch the flit
      Of evening kiss, sent dancing on the sheen
Wavelet from out the bosom of the sky,
   Refluent from the chaste and argent lips
      Of Cupid's own charming pride, the night queen.

XXXII.

From among the glittering hosts, which, like
   Lost meteors seemed, we looked and saw our own
      World roll away 'mid gold stars to take
Its place in the clear blue vaults, as a night
   Gem in the crown of Heaven, in honor, worn,
      Of the day-god, whose reign will never break.

XXXIII.

Broke the voice of Night, on the great deep, in
   Silver strains, so bewitching, soft and slow,
      That our minds went out in charmed reveries;
And our hearts were drunken with joy within,
   To hear rhythmes of the deep so sweet and low,
      Sending back their wild and wierd symphonies.

XXXIV.

On, we went, as trained mariners in the
  Great ocean of space, smoothly flying. Where
  Ere we looked, the scowling visage of Darkness
Was confronting us. The stars, we could see,
  Were growing smaller, and the glowing sphere.
  Named the sun, seemed to be dark and sightless.

XXXV.

Like ærolites roll'd we through ether
  Frare and dark. Up, or down, we knew not,
  So gentle our wing that inclinations
On us made no impression, and whither
  Going we could not discern, as a dot
  Of golden hue the world our calculations.

XXXVI.

Thwarted, and lost we were on the tideless waste
  Of space: lost, amid the twirl of strange worlds.
  And system of worlds we knew not of.
Our own loved birth of spheroid had been displaced
  And from our longing vision strayed. (8) The twirls
  Of immensity seemed, alike, far off.

XXXVII.

In the depths behind, we could not discern
  His face from golden specks of other worlds.
  From view disappearing. All darker grew,
As our wingless flight went on. How to learn
  Where we were, or how the nebula whirls
  About in troubled gnarls, we did not know.

XXXVIII.

Star after star dim grew and disappeared:
  The mother of darkness, dense, we could feel
  As her sable folds about us hung; lo !
Our easy flight went on to where feared
  Some bourne dreadful to me: I could not wheel
  About, for back again I could not go.

XXXIX.

I knew from whence we came, but did not know
  Whither going: but yet our flight went on:
  In circles, curves or tangents I knew not.
Where ere I looked, or our course might go
  But murky blackness fill'd the dreadful throng
  On us weighing, too ominous now for doubt.

XL

All seems one vast cimmerian cave;
　No light flits its wing across the sable face;
　　No waking sound stirs the fountain of the deep.
Death over this vast universal grave
　Has spread his veil and left no lingering trace
　　Of life.　All is darkness, hush'd, asleep!

XLI.

I could not speak from fright, or sign, converse
　As mutes.　But my thoughts in thunder spoke. we
　　Are lost, and will not again the glowing
Face of the sun, or the bright universe,
　The grandeur again of its visage, see.
　　All the while the blackness, more black was growing.

XLII.

The heart flutter of despair in my breast
　As if never knit, I felt; the unmoved mists
　　Of eternity, the father and mother
Of all horror threw around me the test
　Of despair, intensified by the lists
　　Around, now too dark to see each other.

CANTO II.

I.

On an immense cloud we sat, of darkness,
　While stillness mark'd the awful depths about us.
　　Locked in the unmoved breast of immensity—
Hushed was the very shadow of blackness,
　So still that I could hear the ebb and gush
　　Of nerve, flash in its intensity.

II.

Our own thoughts we could hear, for expression
　Wreathing within the portals of the head,
　　As they rushed upon us the gasp of gloom
Intensified our woe.　Extinction
　Of ourselves could not be.　There were no dead
　　Memories there. or records of a tomb.

III.

Proclus sat mute; I tried to revile
　For bringing on us this terrible ban;
　　But I could not. I knew he did what he could.

The fates, I remember, gave us a smile,
A boding most ill for the manes of a man.
As we passed the bounds of the world's sisterhood.

IV.

I thought as I sat in grief, half dreaming,
I saw through the black locks of Erebus.
The flash of whose eyes a darker dark shade
Threw on the scene most real and seeming,
A lone being fast coming toward us,
She seemed a crippled and shriveled old jade.

V.

I wondered her coming; though from her look
I doubted her friendship, or good design.
Approaching, she touched, with her long finger.
The crown of each head, though not a word spoke
She, but from her distaff a silken line
Thread she spun, most delicate and slender.

VI.

"My errand you wish," our visitor said
Giving her spindle a terrible turn;
"The manes I spin for are immortal: so
I'm spinning for you, life's endless thread, (I)
For death you wish, and ever may yearn,
But who remains here finds woe upon woe."

VII.

Giving her spindle another great turn
She spun a fine thread prodigiously long.
"To heed of my work, my name you should know.
The gods all revere me, humanity yearn
For my smiles and thread, with anthems and song
Sound loud the praise of the sister of Clotho."

VIII.

For us no change! E'en Death, sweet messenger
Of Peace, come not will to bring us relief!
Here for all eternity. Oh! sad, sad
Thought! We, in this thrall for aye must linger
On and live,—live for what? Ah! the dregs of grief:
With no hope, e'en of death, to make us glad.

IX.

Swell a drooping heart. Oh! Death, thou benign
Leveler of men and all things terene:

3

That we may comprehend thy amplitude
To heal the ills of flesh, the wrongs of mind,
And all the anguish of the heart unseen
Smother'd in the breast's deep solitude;

X.

And let upon each brow be writ,
Death, man's dearest friend, linger and live
That we may die, and dying, leave behind
Those combinations of heart-aches which sit
Upon the throne of all, to always give
In recompense a promise undefined.

XI.

We there sorrowing sat, gazing into
The thorex of deep Chaos. A faint glim
Far in the murky distance, came crashing thro'
The dark depths of Cimmerius. A new
Hope, sister of Despair, moved me, and when
It a little nearer came, brought to view

XII.

The person of our coming friend, so fair,
That the fervent kiss of Morn, flush from the
Rosy lips of Aurora, messenger queen
Of health, heaven and love, still lingered there
And revel'd in that pure felicity,
Felt when sweet Hope frowns on Despair, I ween

XIII.

For all this time Procleus had not spoke;
Between his two hands, held he, his bow'd head:
His eyes, like piercing darts into the deep
Gloom, sent a steady, intent look, unbroke
By the rolling folds of the great deep dead
Night, around whose life lay eternal sleep.

XIV.

"What wist thou, Procleus friend? So close thou.
In meditation art. Seest not the glim,
In yonder dark void, ploughing the misty
Deep, as a bird of lucid wing on the brow
Of Time coming, swiftly?" I asked of him.
He then arousing, looked most wistfully.

XV.

He, up springing, said: "To think is to be." (2)

I sat and thought of Vesta, morning gleam
    Of hope: and, at last her bright face illum'd
My soul. I saw it afar. Lost were we..
    And I sent hunting through the spacious vesne
    Of earth my thoughts, intense, and, very soon

XVI.

Across the bosom of the deep, I saw
    Glimpse the thought voice of Vesta, fairest one
    Of the celestial throng. To bring her
Was to think intensely. This is the law, (3)
    The astral, through electric thought must run
    The wires spun from the complex woof of air.

XVII.

The flesh is seen streaking the vaults of space.
    The thought, electric, strikes the fragile nerves:
    And, as a subtle flash through space unseen,
Comes the ministering friend as in the race
    Of time. As a kind friendly spirit serves
    Your wants and needs, in many ways, I ween.

XVIII.

She, the fairest wanderer, like a great
    Ball, phosphoric, by some grim monster,
        Through the bowels of darkness shot, came to
Us, and by tongueless impression. "What fate
    Hither sent you hath?" she said. "Who sponsor
        Came, the universe again would know you?"

XIX.

"Know ye not, that when the pleiades
    Ye pass'd and turned your backs upon the face,
        Fair and blooming, of Arcturus, and into
The Arcana, you would penetrate, these
    Dark, fathomless abodes of night, to trace
        Again your flight was difficult to do?"

XX.

"Pray, chide us not! With our folly intense,
    That induced us to hither come and leave
        The fair earth, with all its glow and grandeur.
Turning, twirling, changing without offense
    Among the constellations of worlds and weave
        Its rhomb'd path on and around, forever:

XXI.

Forever and forever, on around
  Among its kindred spheroids, unswerving,
    Undeviating from its course in the
Trackless expanse of space. Well, we have found
  Our folly," said Procleus, "Deserving
    Of punishment somewhat. Pray, where are we?"

XXII.

"Where is the end of this, the mother of
  Darkness?" The basement, or dome, of this vast
    Prison house, erst to us unknown; and thou
Vesta fair, messenger, swift from off
  The Plutonian shore, here with us cast.
    Our presence chide, on night's eternal brow."

XXIII.

"Oh! Frowning Chaos, speak and tell us where
  The end is, and periphery of space!
    And bear us hence to life and light, again."
Vesta then replied: "The wings of morning fair,
  That bear afar the sweet and glowing face
    Of day, could not, while Time's limitless reign

XXIV.

Breathes on matin song, soft and mellow,
  Its symphonious strains, a beginning
    Make in space, whose vast vastness no center
Has. No end, top, side, base. One great fellow
  Of eternal spread is hers. All the spinning
    Spheres that play within its bosom, enter

XXV.

"Not one atom's size in space eternal.
  Could you upon the wings of lightning ride
    And make that ride forever on and on.
While the glowing sun in his supernal
  Grandeur sends vivifying rays through th' tide
    Of time, space still lies on, yet, farther on.

XXVI.

"On the pinions of thought could you astride
  Be placed, with might to instantaneous
    The worlds around traverse: and thus on speed.
Till the stars fall, the moon wane and the tide
  Cease pulsation, earth to extraneous
    Matter pass, not e'en a start will you ha' made

XXVII.

"In boundless, incomprehensible space,
The one ubiquity. The all of all—
That only which embraces ev'ry where,
And all things. Upon whose all-spreading face
Is the image, the impress and the call
Of that which now is, was, or ever were."

XXVIII.

Lit up the face of Vesta, a calm smile,
And looking away, she, in a whisper said,
Which, from the dense stillness surrounding us
Seem'd as an explosion, on the deep file
Of night, artillery-like, in contests dead
Of foes. "I'll guide you beyond Erebus."

XXIX.

"Tarry not! We will haste, our journey make
And wave our hands again across the brow
Of morning, and freight her bosom grand,
With our presence and once again awake
To the smiles of Mira, feel the glow
Of Eta flush by light eternal, fan'd.

CANTO III.

I.

Hope! home!! love and heaven!!! Links divine,
That span the yawning gulf of despair
And lead man on to results great and grand,
Despite himself. Fleet on the wings of Time
We rode from Chaos to regions more fair,
That pointed to our home, our father-land.

II.

Vesta was to Procleus the sagess
Whose words were wisdom, and decision, law:
As down a long, lambent stream of light we
Sped our way. To me, her looks were pages
Of expressive love, on whose lips, with awe
I dwelt my thoughts, with true felicity.

III.

We sped away, as on a stream, we were,
Of light, which bore us on in hope afar
To a distant world, in whose stellar dome
Seem'd other laughing worlds, some near, some far.

Wore some an azure hue, and there a star
  Twinkling bright beneath us, a smile would own. (1)

IV.

Around, above, below, before, behind,
  Peeping through ether frore and blue,
    Bright-eyed spheroids seem'd to hang and watch us.
The while, Vesta, our fair chaperone, kind
  And attentive, gave of her travels true
    Account and led us on in discourse, thus:

V.

"On yonder bright hanging orb I've sat
  And for hours watched the living, moving
    Throng that are born, live and die on its face.
As mortals are born, live and die on that
  Sphere called earth.   A more gentle and loving
    Folk could not be than that small stellar race.

VI.

Upon the pure ambient air they live,
  And, breathe from off ambrosial sweetness,
    Life exquisite.   Like the lithe humming bird,
That flits from flower to flower to give
  A kiss refining to their completeness,
    This folk flit on the air, unwing'd, unheard.

VII.

Small, they, not larger than an infant seem,
  Plump, yet lighter than the air on which they float,
    Or ride upon, in graceful attitudes,
In zephyr-like playfulness.   On a treen
  Of air they sit at times, and themselves gloat
    To fullness on its sweet beatitudes.

VIII.

There is no object more to them, in life,
  Than that of flirting with the goddess fair
    Of pleasure.   They will court no other meed
Or wist for other things, for all is rife
  To completeness.   All the surroundings rare
    Of joy, are there, without the guile of greed.

IX.

Breath to them is meathe and food as to the
  Lungs is air to sentient beings of earth.
    Ailments are to them and to theirs unknown.

They have the felicitudes of all the free
  Wing'd glories, chaste and true, brought by the birth
  Of perfect living, in times long since flown.

X.

They are the types of perfect beings, in
  A perfect world: and, where perfection is,
  Reigns true felicity.   Not all alike
Are these world orbs: galling sin
  Revels on the face of some with his
  Tooth of virus always prepar'd to strike.

XI.

Some are propagating worlds.   Mira,
  There, in swelling brightness hangs, (2) with her, springs
  From out the depths of life perennial.
The primal germs that succeed the fiery
  Epoch of her being, which to her clings.

XII.

To Casseopavia's grandeur we'll fly:
  There Ticho Brahe drank the wonders in. (3)
  And from the blaze effulgent that did gleam
Upon him from the deep and tongueless sky,
  He learned to love the truths: which was to him
  But the glimmering of a fretful dream.

XIII.

As we sped on lightning's lurid wing, through
  Perfect light, in the distance far we saw
  The earth: around which a semi-opaque
Substance lay, deeper, it appeared to view,
  Than mortal eye could fathom.   There the law
  Of optics lost its force: and to our wake

XIV

Of eye, above the terene scenes of grand
  And sublime realities, typified
  The wildest imaginings.   It was the
Periphery of air substance.(4)   The hand
  Of nature placed outside of the outer side
  Of this air ocean of intensity

XV.

An inert, hollow and transparent sphere.
  Mountains towering.   There plains and meads
  Cours'd by rivers, cut by streams of lesser

Verge. Here spread a silver lake, there a meer, (5)
  With blushing flowerets around its leads
    Of beauty. I was made a confessor

XVI.

Of my own errors. Fragrance sweet
  Pervaded the highest heights. The soul meets
    Its awe. Here grace of varied tints presents
A beauty, the grandest mind must own. Fleet
  On the wings of thought, the clinge face speaks
    In volumes of its majestic pleasance.

XVII.

While yet I thought, to those vast bounds we hied,
  And, by a cool and placid meer we stood,
    Fringed it was with a sward dense, and branching trees.
In its pearly depths and along its side
  Hung shadows of the far-upreaching wood,
    Whose broad leaves rustled in the wafting breeze.

XVIII.

In the precincts of Devachan were cast. (6)
  It rests on the periphery of the air,
    Which as dense to manes as is earth to man,
Like water to penetrate. Cities, vast
  With apures of beauty, excessive far,
    To man's conceptions in his wildest plan.

XIX.

Beneath, we saw the rolling earth, her sides
  Turn to our look. We saw men there, and beasts
    Wade the fluid air, the earth surrounding.
We saw men sicken and die, and the tides
  Of life change and rechange, in order. Feasts
    Of death were about. We saw life bounding.

XX.

Fading and changing. There many we saw
  Succumb to the inevitable. The
    Manas lighter than the damp, sluggish air, (7)
Would leave the rupa and arise through the law (8)
  Of Karma, if from the animal were free,
    To th' sphere of Devachan beautiful, fair.

XXI.

'Twas morn, unlike the earth. The orient,
  In argent sheen bestow'd her smile; and, man

Awoke: not from his sleepy dreams to plod
Through life along, with sly and vile intent
  To thrawl his fellow with galling ban
Of servitude. Neither to find a god

XXII

Seclusive to dull ignorance, sublime,
  That has for aye made "countless millions mourn,"
    But with matin songs and pleasing smiles 'woke
Fair nature with a deep and rhythmic chime
  Of love, on whose dulcet strains is borne
    Th' word "Fraternity" untainted, unbroke.

XXIII.

Upon a craggy height and visne quite near,
  Disport maidens with agile beasts of prey.
    The condor swims above, and sports the dove
Around as minnerets in brooklets clear.
  Here all are friends; all are pets. The day
    Of greed has pass'd and here all live in love.

XXIV.

On yonder quivering lake, whose silver
  Wavelets each other chase—they come, they go—
    Like argent streamlets from some stellar sun
Dressed in animated grace to smile. Never
  Into madden'd billows made. A faint glow
    Like blazing zephyrs, through its bosom run.

XXV.

From the deep center to its golden verge
  Is its laughing face blent with crystalline,
    While diamoned tippets kiss each gentle spray:
And wavelets play upon the deep, nor serge
  The bosom of the placid meer serene,
    But all in concord move in grand display.

XXVI.

Blooms th' syringa and scents the scene with love,
  Birds, sportive, sing, and beasts in friendship play.
    The voice of man, in euphonious rhymes
Strikes the diapason of the spheres above,
  And music cheers the heart, as day follows day,
    And blends into one like heaven-born chimes.

XXVII.

Here lay flowery dells. There run canons deep.
  Leap streams refreshing from the mountain sides:

4

Great rivers, tranquil, move themselves along,
Here man, in sylvan shades, finds calm retreat,
The queen of night in argent trosseau rides
In grace sublime amid this stellar throng.

XXVIII.

Before our eyes, fascinated with scenes
Most bewitching, beauty locked in beauty,
 Lay. The sky, deep-toned a mellow refrain
Back sent to the 'wilder'd eye, with its gleams
Of grandeur, from spheres afar. Here duty
 Wrapped in nature gave love its spacious reign.

XXIX.

While thinking, if in bewilderment we
Can think, a stately youth, messuivent
 From Procheana, the principal mart
Where Eta blends her ruddy smiles, mild, free
And enchanting; with Mira's blushes, blent
 With green and white, from Sirius' heart,

XXX.

Came up the golden strand, wash'd by waters clear
From dew-drops still'd on blooms ambrosial
 By jeweled eyes of matin stars. His hand
A sapphire plate, held, quaintly wrought and queer.
What his errand, stately was, could not tell
 We, but knew it must be from high command.

XXXI.

In the plate a note of finest texture
Was, inviting us to Procheana
 As favorite guests from the royal household
Of Amchus. A favorable answer
Was hoped for. The while low-trill'd hosannah
 From a thousand tongues sweetly-cadenc'd, roll'd.

XXXII.

A convoy of a hundred shallops came,
Adorned with silken sails of varied hues,
 With keels of pearls to cut the tranquil sea.
From each mast, gib and yard, St. Almo's flame
Afforded light to guide the nymphian crews
 That bent with main against the drifting lea.

XXXIII.

Holy love, offspring of Nervana, swell'd

My breast, as the beam of day bursted forth
And we betook ourselves aboard the gay
Nymphia. Above a mellow haze dwell'd;
Upon the scene, stars from the crystal north
Sent smiles of joy to help us on our way.

XXXIV.

Latona breath'd a gentle waft, and moved
Upon the lay of transparent waters,
Our gay bark, with nymphan beauty vying.
Holy were my thoughts, by heart approved,
In those moments of ecstacies. Daughters
Of young love bent on us smiles undying.

XXXV.

Stepping aboard the shallop, frail craft
Of transparent keel, and sails of zephyr
Cloth outspread. Our eyes looked on the inner
Orb. Our earth, which we could see as we had left
It in its sombre hue, did not differ
Much from yore, except it seem'd some dimmer.

XXXVI.

As view'd from the great outside station; that
Man knows not as he wades his liquid deep.
In the ethereal water of our
Visne of outer spread, swims the minneret
And other playful sports. The rapid sweep
Of dolphins and larger fish of power,

XXXVII.

All gambol'd in concord and harmony.
Far away in the dim and azure distance,
Arose mountains, naze, jetting crags and peaks
So clear and transparent, our sight their way
Did not obstruct. The eye, no resistance
They gave. Through all the ken of material sweep

XXXVIII.

Above the zenith, a spire gleam'd in
The distance, in the course we going were.
Alolius low and sweet sent us greeting
Symphonius. A city appear'd within
Our ken, of crystal white; ev'rywhere
The voice of beauty our eyes came greeting.

xxxix.

Procheana lingered on ev'ry lip,
  On every brain daguerreotyped
    Was this peerless princess of beauty.   Light
Grew every heart.   All the ellin ships
  Dip'd their standards of argent stars and striped
    Vermilion, marine blue and spotless white.

xl.

A convoy met us on sylphan wing, and
  On balmy breaths of ambrosial bloom,
    We rode.   Amchus gave us welcome.   We felt
The presence of perfection about.   Grand,
  Simple and unique.   Press'd on us the noon
    Of sublimity.   Here, completeness dwelt.

xli.

Joy reigned, and ev'ry soul th' beatitude
  Of pleasure owned.   Grand edifices of
    Tinsel'd growth and frost-like frescos clear
And bewitching, shaded the magnitude
  Of taste exquisite.   Sounded afar off
    The silver chime.   Welcome, most welcome here.

xlii.

It is all one pleasure here, we felt.   "No,"
  Amchus replied, knowing our inmost thought:
    "This is viata fair, the pure of earth life
Only here obtains.   On the plane below
  The real of grosser life to the view brought
    More plainly is.   There, the crude and coarse are rife.

xliii.

Here folk of pure behave and walk, feed on
  Thoughts harmonious and guide the mind to
    Flights felicitous; as mirthful birds their
Throats attune to melody, music and song
  Impart enchantments to the depths of true
    Coarage, and bear us to achievments rare.

xliv.

Spring blooms eternal here.   The years roll on.
  Morning appears sweetly with her smiles
    Outspread.   Evening lingers on the stars around
And lends to night a golden cast along
  Its way.   Up here, no thought untrue defiles
    The place, to wreck our inmost grace profound.

XLV.

Confounded with the concatenations
  Of beauty, celestial, there upon my
  Frail senses obtruded, I stood aghast,
And wondered if all those grand potations
  Were for my credulity; or, if I
  Truly saw, and if they should always last?

XLVI.

I see, but cannot comprehend.   I hear,
  But do not understand.   I feel, and still   ‑
  My senses are deluded.   :"Where are we?"
I asked.   "Look ye beneath your feet in clear
  Observation, you may behold the fill
  Of your great wonder.   There, what do you see?"

XLVII.

Great Amchus said.   I looked, in beauty sheen
  Beneath the zephyr of my feet there lay
  Our own Columbia, with her rivers,
Lakes, mountains, plains, cities.   She smil'd the queen
  Of all the earth.   There bloom'd the face of day
  In all its glory of great endeavors.

XLVIII.

Pulsated through its steel-bound arteries
  The commerce of the land.   Sang from the loom,
  The mill, the field, the forge, the office and
The shop, the song of thrift; realities
  Of intellectual endowment; the groom
  And the bride, fruit of the brain and honest hand.

XLIX.

There stand the Sierras, Rockies, the Wahsateh,
  With their cowls of snow and bowels of gold,
  Ribs of silver, frames of adamant and
Iron hard; coal to smelt them and a catch
  Of lead, with all the useful metals told
  To commerce, in profusion rich and grand.

L.

There spreads away through many thousand miles
  Rich plains, alluvial, that groan beneath
  The plowman's sturdy tread and golden grain:
There laugh and work, a goodly folk, and smiles
  The lap of luxury that wist bequeath
  To honest toil, the harvest feast again.

LI.

From the golden lap of the Pacific shore
  To the laved rocks of Atlantic's verge;
    From Rio Del Norte to the ice girth bound
Of Alaska, lie inviting, in store
  For man, all the needs that nature can urge
    Or, in reason express, there may be found

LII.

Dotting the plains and outspread land,
  Homes, orchards, vineyards and capacious farms;
    Towns and villas neat, cities with their wealth,
Look up thro' noble efforts to the grand
  Achievements of the day, and with their charms
    Enchant the eye of enterprise and health.

LIII.

There floats the grandest sight of all, the pride
  Of ev'ry loyal heart, as well the charm
    Of ev'ry eye. The old flag that long ago
Wav'd at Yorktown, and, was the faithful guide
  In eighteen twelve. It proudly nerv'd the arm
    Of victory in the fields of Mexico.

LIV.

That grand old flag! That blessed flag!! that waved
  In triumph o'er so many sanguine fields.
    The pride of Lincoln, Grant and Washington.
Waves now in triumph, as it always wav'd.
  In proud defiance, and it never yields
    In the hands of a true and noble son.

LV.

Bless'd is the man who finds a shelter 'neath
  The smiles of that old flag! Who is anxious
    For its weal. Blessed is the mind that finds a
Home for spirits pure within their belief!
  As guides thro' the dark and sombre meshes
    Of earth life, to a brighter, fairer day.

LVI.

Who feels the spirit hosts about him, guides
  Gentle true of life: who notes their kind
    Endeavors to lead him on, if they can,
Where joy of halcyon years survives the tides
  Of Time severe: where the angel world combine
    In wish to make of each a true man.

LVII.

Man! Strange combination. He acts! He lives!!
 Struggle of the past; blossom of the present:
  Fruit of the future; child of the forces:
Offspring of all the past; the source that gives
 Expression to all that which is pleasant,
  Grand, good and holy. His great thought courses

LVIII.

The universal cause, and carries back
 To primeval plentitudes the fond mind,
  That it may drink of its own far back birth,
To volume on the future that reflect
 Of thought that comes again in force to bind
  Him to heaven when unfettered by earth.

CANTO IV.

I.

For yourselves, fair Vesta, you may accept
 The courtesies proffered by great Amchus,
  And grace Procheana with your presence,
Longer, please. Bear great Amchus my regret—
 My stay I feel is short; and feeling thus,
  My liking draws me to the vista hence.

II.

Adieu! me bid my friends, and, I was left
 On the shores of lake Mamora which lay
  By the wash'd feet of Mount Kaarah, whose brow
Kiss'd the furtive clouds that pass'd by: and, cleft
 Their aqueous wings of sun-distilled spray.
  As food for verdue in the vales below.

III.

For hours. Ah! there are no hours here.
 A day is like a moment. fleet of wing.
  When one can stand alone and feast his eyes
And fill his soul on beauties ev'rywhere.
 I felt as if the morning heart of spring
  Was here, with all its flush of pure emprise.

IV.

There spread an esplanade its sward of green
 Before a temple made of flowers gay:
  And sang sweet songsters of an airy wing
In notes soprano to the brooklet's sheen.

That broke in accents o'er their pebbled way
And left behind to laugh, the mountain spray.

v.

In the heathery deep, the cushat's song
Swell'd the notes of Mavis on the ambient air.
The stately buck his shadow in the stream
Beholds with pride; and, through the mountain rang
Echos loud, from the lion in his lair,
And bleating lambs answered back the panther's scream.

vi.

A mellow gray from Ursa Minor spread,
Upon the sky cerulean and clear,
A grand relief, and, Sirius, a glad
Morning kiss sent to the proud mountain head.
And lap'd a silver fold across the meer
And wav'd with Mira on the verge, a plaid.

vii.

"Is this real? Can there be one thing more
To sweet existence added, to make complete
The beatitude of man?" Thus, through my mind
Ran the thought without meditation. Before
An answer to my 'quiring mind came, fleet
Of foot tripped a maid and said in tones kind:

viii.

"I saw your wistful thought across the disk
Of heaven fly, and in response I came
To bear the answer to yourself alone.
It is not mete that one of earth should risk
His happiness alone. It takes the flame
Of love to make heaven e'en a pleasant home.

ix.

One may traverse the face of heaven wide,
And drink the joys of all its beauties in.
Yet, sad within his heart a void must be,
If there be not one lingering by his side,
Or close around with loving words for him.
And for that love, get love as full and free.

x.

Heaven, with all its joys and its pleasures,
With all its sweets and lavish'd beauty grand.
With its infinitude of glories true

Will sink into sameness, and its treasures
Vanish as the dew of morn at the sun's command.
　　If they are not observed and loved by two."

XI.

Without further say, the damsel smiling left
Me on the strand; and with her went my heart
　　And all the fullness of the beautiful
Surroundings, which lay barren and bereft
Of soul; though unchang'd. they could not impart
　　That refreshing glow. they erst had so well.

XII.

Sitting down upon an emerald sward
My heart went back. I bow'd my head
　　And thought of Hester. loved and left behind.
In my earnest soul her loved voice. I heard,
In expressive grief. I was dead.
　　She alone was left, and to fate resigned.

XIII

And, I said. "Is this death?" The elysian shore.
The great dreaded hereafter? Or is this
　　The dream of death, sister of extinction?
What is death, that his visits should be more
Than the sweet creeping sleep of bliss,
　　To whose arms all yield without distinction?

XIV

Is not death our greatest boon, our dearest friend.
Walking the earth, spreading benedictions
　　To the millions? To the weary relief,
To the burden'd sweet rest? It is the end
Of all sorrow, all troubles. all afflictions;
　　It makes all sadness short: all sorrows brief.

XV

It dulls famine's sharp and ravaging tooth;
It cools the fever'd brow. and lays the hand
　　Upon the frore breath of night;
At the last moment, joy to the beggar's roof:
And all the languishing poor of the land
　　Find in the grand sleep of death, a pure delight.

XVI

Wherever life goes with his long red train
Of afflictions, death is present ever,
　　With his smiles and his relief; be it where

Eternal frost, ice and snow, their refrain
　　Of tortured existence broadcasts, or whether
　　　In the tropics with their dense and fetid air.

XVII.

Or if on the mountain top, or the deep
　　Below, upon the arid plain, or where
　　　The Mango blooms, or in the jungles wild,
Death, conquering king, with eternal sleep
　　Bathes the brow and soothes the pain'd heart with care.
　　　Brings peace to all, the aged and the child.

XVIII.

Death has no special visne or favor'd clime;
　　His is the reign of that eternal spread
　　　That pervades the universe with the serge
Of life.　He rides upon the brow of Time
　　Spreading through all space his unnumber'd dead.
　　　Making all the living his 'special targe.

XIX.

And when the kiss of death has brought repose,
　　And we are number'd with that solemn bourne
　　　That bears us hence, the living still will ask:
"What next?"　The candid answer, "No one knows."
　　From behind this sad scene all light hath flown,
　　　Comes then the joy of Hope whose pleasant task

XX.

It is, to lead cold reason through the gloom,
　　Of which sophists speak and poets have sung;
　　　Kings, statesmen, philosophers, wise and learn'd.
Alike have stood begging at the tomb,
　　For some echo back.　But, alas! its tongue
　　　Is hush'd, and Hope alone brings the return.

XXI.

Musing thus, I felt the wage of calm sleep
　　Coming, with its lullaby of rest;
　　　I thought the last thought of Hester and home.
How long I slept, the secret angels keep,
　　But I can now measure my feelings best
　　　When my eyes beheld my own native wone.

XXII.

Hard by upon a rising knoll, amid
　　Evergreens, flowers, shrubs and branching trees

A cemetery was. I sped my way thither
And felt relief with the ramble. Was hid,
  In trailing vines and shrubs of various leaves,
  Many graves that nameless will be ever.

XXIII.

Amid this city of unnumber'd dead
A gathering, large, of people I observed; ·
  I will'd to saunter up to view the crowd.
When close approached, I heard a hymnal read
And saw the cortege grave, and a reserved,
  Sad look on each face, the humble and the proud.

XXIV.

I walked among them, no one seem'd to see
  Me. Though I spoke to many, no one seem'd
To hear. Was sung a mournful plaint, sad, low
And impressive there; and, with gravity,
A man of eloquence, being esteemed
  For sublimity and linguistic flow,

XXV.

Chain'd the audience with a wordy spell
  Of the man before him dead. And I heard
Things that stirr'd my soul with admiration
Of the life of him who in silence lay. Well
Tim'd were the sentences, and fell the word
  Of praise that fill'd one with animation.

XXVI.

"I came not here to speak in fulsome praise
  O'er the bier of a man I knew to admire:
  But my testimony of him to give
As he was in life. Scarce had he the days
Of youth thrown off and the station higher
  Of manhood assumed, when he ceased to live.

XXVII.

But already hewn he had himself a name,
  Not in the field of human woe or blood,
  Nor by the prowess won through wanton pain.
His was a higher and a grander fame,
A fame that lives among the great and good,
  That all admire, but very few attain.

XXVIII.

Too great he was to do another wrong:

Too proud to lie; too noble to deceive:
  All men he loved; and in his heart no guile
He bore. He help'd the weak and curbed the strong;
  His hand was ever ready to relieve
    Distress. The world he greeted with a smile.

XXIX.

For those who had wrong'd him he did not ask
  To have forgiven, but he them forgave;
    Malice, no lodgment found in his pure mind:
For him to do good was his wish and task;
  He lived and spoke the truth, and was a brave
    Defender of right of every kind.

XXX.

A genial and a generous friend   ,
  Would practice no deceit. He hated guile.
    His words upon a golden thread were strung.
And in a weft did all the virtues blend:
  Nor would he wrong doings guild with a smile.
    Or ply a vile or a deceitful tongue.

XXXI.

He knelt before no god or fancied throne;
  No sect, priest or christ, claim'd his devoirs:
    He scorn'd the tyrant and his galling ban:
He worshiped but the good in man alone,
  In his heart abhorred what virtue abhors,
    And saw in man the true Savior of man."

XXXII.

I thought this man, once lived, but now is dead
  I cannot doubt. One fact impresses me:
    Man, his praises are too late in giving.
How much better, far, that good things be said
  While sensuous is the subject, that he
    Might somewhat be encouraged while living.

XXXIII.

But 'tis the rule, be it with regrets said,
  Good men are curs'd and life is render'd sore
    Through menial, jealous censurings
Which never close until the man is dead,
  Then lavish is the tongue to blandish o'er
    His name with most extravagant sayings.

XXXIV.

My absence may be counted yet by days,
 My boyhood friends are here, and yet alive,
   But from my knowledge I cannot recall
The one entitled to this lavish praise.
 I dare say, should the dead one now revive,
   He would not know who the speaker meant at all.

XXXV.

"A little lower he must have been than
 The angels," I thought, and while pondering
   My eyes fell on a female, bowed in deep
Grief, by the casket. I marvel'd; but when
 Her eyes, suffused with tears upturned, pleading
   That he was not dead, but in a deep sleep,

XXXVI.

I saw the sad, but most beautiful face
 Of Hester. The love of my love. The charm
   Of my charm. The soul of my soul. My all.
I hastened and did with love embrace
 Her lithe and waning waist with my strong arm,
   But she heeded me not, and yet did call

XXXVII.

Upon the scarf'd and crape-clad ministers
 Of good to forego the task and deliver
   To her for a defined time, the keeping
Of the casket. She knelt in prayer, and with tears
 Streaming her cheeks, said: "Oh! will I never
   See you my Philo?" moaned she, still weeping.

XXXVIII.

"I am by your side dear, look up," I said,
 But yet she heeded me not. I kissed the
   Brimming tear; and, endearing words I spoke
To her. Still in prayer she called my name. Fled
 From her recognition have I, yet she
   Calls Philo; and, in that name did invoke

XXXIX.

Ministering spirits of love for aid.
 I pitied her and on her cheeks again
   Impress'd a kiss, and spoke words endearing
Again of assured love. In prayer she said.

As though her heart would break with grief and pain,
"He is not dead, Oh ! give me a hearing."

XL.

"Grant me this one boon, Oh ! sexton, I pray,
Open once more the cruel casket that I
May again bend on his lovely face mine eyes
Before the cold earth, the immortal day,
Of my love drink in, that I then may die
With his last lovely smile upon me." Surprise

XLI.

Struck me dumb, when in the casket I saw
That which was myself, asleep. The earth bound
Part. "To think is to be and thoughts are things."
Joy took the place of grief. The grave's dark maw
Was unrequited. Hester embraced, found
Solace in the heart, where love eternal springs.

NOTES ON HESTER AND PHILO.
CANTO I.
XI.

(1)   "My senses were alive."

Oft times persons lying in a state of suspended animation, or in a trance state, hear and know everything that is going on around them, but have no power of making their condition known; and, not unfrequently, persons have been buried alive, when, in fact, they were but in a deep trance.

There lives a lady in Davenport, Iowa, who became ill, and to all appearances departed this life. She was robed for the bridal chamber of death, and her funeral was going on, when signs of life were observed. The eyes of mourning were changed to anxiety: then to rejoicing, for she was restored. Afterwards she married a prominent physician who is now, (1890) living happily with his wife, and following his profession in Davenport, Iowa.

This is only one of thousands of instances of suspended animation. In cholera times, and during great epidemics, such cases are frequent. There lived a man in Indiana who was honored with a large funeral. An eloquent minister preached the funeral sermon every, word of which he heard, but could make no reply. The last leave was taken of him, and he was placed in the hearse and the cortege was proceeding to the place of interment, when the driver heard a knocking in the coffin. They stopped for an investigation, to find the dead man able to sit up. He lived many years afterwards.

People lying in a trance state often hear and know everything that is going on about them, but have not the power to move a muscle and make their condition known.

A lady once, whom I knew in life, had become very ill and swooned away to a state of trance. She grew cold and pulseless. Her friends thought her dead. She was laid out, dressed in the bridal robes of death, and laid in the casket for burial. She knew everything that was going on, but was powerless to make them know that she was not dead. Signs of life were accidentally observed in her. She was taken from the casket and restored to life.

XVII.

(2) ·'There in the deep voice of solitude
       Adepts of the black art abide in caves.''

There is, connected with the Buddhistic religion, an order known as Adepts. They belong to a Brotherhood of which the Mahatmas, are of a higher degree. They profess to have acquired great knowledge in physic power. To acquire this learning the adept retires to the Himalayas and there the neophyte places himself in a most rigid condition of training, which he must continue for not less than seven years before he can be admitted to the lowest degree of the Brotherhood in occultism, and the probation may extend *ad libitum*. He has no security that he will ever be advanced to the higher knowledge.

The life of the adept requires absolute physical purity. For all the years of probation he must be perfectly chaste, perfectly abstemious and indifferent to physical luxury of every kind. He must train his mind to absolute control and oneness of concentration in thought power. It must rest above all menial things and delve into the occult mysticisms of the latent powers of nature. Through long training and earnest application it is said the adepts have the power to take the astral body from the physical and with the rapidity of thought traverse space and return to life again. The adepts have acquired the science of mental telegraphy that enables them to converse with each other while hundreds and even thousands of miles apart.

XXI.

(3) "Again to chaos whose habitation
      Is the catalysis of cosmic mists."

There was a time when there was no earth, moon, sun or stars. Yet the matter that compose them always existed and will never have an ending. Before the world combination was effected by the mutual attraction of particles of matter, those particles were in a state of cosmic mist. Darkness prevaded the deep, and chaos (which is simply an unorganized state) reigned.

This atomic mist was matter, and each little atom contained the elements of force called attraction, repulsion, life, intelligence, spirit, all of which in after periods were made manifest according to the aggregation and combination of material substances.

There is no dead matter in the universe. Everything that is, was, or ever will be, has life, and also intelligence, but the life and intelligence of the rock is different from that of the flower or tree. The intelligence of man is different from the intelligence of the brute, just in proportion to the difference of material combination.

XXIV.

(4) "The astral knows no bounds."

It is asserted as a fact, that the spirit often leaves the body of the living man and becomes manifest to observers at great distances from the body. This is partly proven by hypnotic experiments, when the mind of the subject is sent to distant places and then perfectly describe the persons there, the room, furniture and the very conversation of the ones visited, though the hypnotic subject is an absolute stranger to them all.

XXV.

(5) "Our motors were our wills."

The spirit but wills to go, and is there.

XXX.

(6) "We saw, up creeping
      The purple morn, above the orient,
      As evening spread upon the western verge
      A smile."

At the distance of the moon away, an observer could see at the same glance the rising sun and the golden gleams of evening as she bids the day good by.

XXXIV.

(7) "Wherere we looked the scowling visage of darkness
      Was confronting us "

When you get beyond the reflection of son rays upon the earth, it becomes absolutely dark. The mean distance between the earth and the sun is total darkness. We have light upon the earth, because of the stopping of and reflection of the sun's rays.

XXXVII.

(8) "Our own loved birth spheroid had been displaced
      And from our longing vision strayed."

Could we stand upon the face of the moon, we could look out into the stellar depths, and view, of a clear night, a beautiful silver orb, in appearance about thirteen times larger than the moon, as it appears now to us. With delight we would sit and watch its revolutions upon its axis, as it would present her sides of variegated beauty to us. We would see the silver-faced Pacific ocean, then creeping up Asia, Africa, Europe, the Atlantic, and in its turn, America. Should we shift to the planet of Venus, we would behold our globe appearing in the azure sky, like a large bright star, and the moon circulating around her, as a a small speck. We would wonder and admire her beauty as we would see her fly away and lose herself in space in her journey around the sun.

Who knows but we would find a people on Venus, further advanced in the sciences and knowledge than the people of the earth are to-day? Who knows but we would find philosophers and statesmen, orators and poets and a state of refinement in advance of our own earth's times?

CANTO II.

VI.

(1) "I'm spinning for you life's endless thread."

In the Grecian mythology the fates consist of three old women, dressed in robes of white ermine, bordered with purple. They wore chaplets made of wool and interwoven with the flowers of narcissus. Their names were Clotho, Lachesis and Atropos. They were daughters of Nox and Erebus. They controlled the thread of life. Lachesis turned the wheel. Clotho drew out the thread, and this thread endued the wearer with eternal life, unless it was cut by the other sister, Atropos.

XV.

(2) "To think is to be."

According to spirit philosophy, a spirit need but think and the distance is crossed and the thing accomplished, if within the scope of Psychic power.

XVI.

(3) "This is the law.
    The astral through electric thought must run
    The wires spun from the complex woof of air."

Through the art of mental telegraphy, an electric chain is formed and the thought, as an entity, runs the wires to the person communicated with, by means of which the two can converse together, though many miles away.

CANTO III.

III.

(1) "Wore some an azure hue and some a star
    Twinkling bright beneath us a smile would own."

Some of the binary stars are of different colors. In the constellation of Leparis, one star is white, the other deep red. In Sygni, one is yellow, the other blue. In Andromedea, they are orange and green. In some instances they seem to be complementary colors. In such instances, the largest star seems to be ruddy or orange, while the smaller one appears blue or green. This may, in some instances, appear so from the known law of optics that when the retina of the eye is excited by the influence of a bright color, the feebler light would appear to have a complementary color. Thus, in Eta Casseopeia there is the beautiful combination of a large white star and one of a rich, ruddy purple. But, this does not follow that the different colored stars are from complementary effects. Sirius, in olden times, was a ruddy star; now it shines with a pure bright light.

Insulated stars of different colors appear in many parts of the stellar region. Some of them are of deep red color; some bright; some tinged with orange and yellow. But, none of these isolated stars are blue, or green. These colors belong to binary association.

XI.

(2) "Mira There in swelling brightness hangs."

Mira, called "the wonderful star," shines with brilliancy at times as a

star approaching one of the first magnitude; then, it decreases for about three
months until it becomes invisible to the naked eye, to a star of the twelfth
magnitude; it remains so, for about five months; then it gradually grows
into its former size and brilliancy. It takes about 331 days to pass through
these phases.

XII.

(3)   "To Casseopeia's grandeur we will fly
    Where Tycho Brahe drank his wonders in."

The father of the celebrated Tycho Brahe desired his son to study law,
but the stronger inclination of the son was astronomy. His course in life was
decided by the sudden appearance of a temporary star in the constellation of
Casseopeia, in Nov., 1572. As he was returning from his laboratory, about
10 in the evening, his attention was called to a star behind him. A flash of
his eye to Casseopiea, caught a star so brilliant and large that it caused a
shadow from his cane. It came suddenly and remained visible for about six-
teen months, and then it gradually disappeared. This strange phenomena
determined Tycho Brahe to become an astronomer. The same star appeared
in 945, in 1264, and it may be reasonably expected in 1891, or 1892. Its pe-
riodicity seems to be about 319 years.

XIV.

(4)   "It was the periphery of air substance."

The air is a fluid, consisting of two gases, oxygen and nitrogen, in a
state of mechanical mixture, but there is always present a small proportion of
carbonic acid gas and aqueous vapor. It is presumed that the atmosphere
is about forty-five miles deep, from the earth upwards. Outside of the belt
of air surrounding the earth, is a more refined substance, called ether.

XV.

(5)   "Mountains towering, there plains and meads
    Cours'd by rivers, cut by streams of lesser verge."

There is an equilibrium in the interplanetary space, so absolutely secure
from attractive disturbances that large and ponderous bodies rest there in
comparative security, as is demonstrated by the inter-stellar rocks known as
aerolites. Some of these have fallen to the earth, weighing as much as 30,000
pounds. These bodies are very heavy, being about 85 per cent. iron. If
such heavy substances can rest in the boson of ether, beyond the periphery of
the air, why not other substances, structures and compositions less ponder-
able?

XVII.

(6)   "In the precincts of Devachan were cast."

In the Buddhic philosophy there is a state in the transition of the ego
from the earth, or animal condition, to Atma, or pure spirit, called Devachan,
which corresponds to the christian conception of heaven. Devachan is the
condition of absolute felicity. Avitchi is just the reverse. There are no moments of enjoyment in Avitchi, no thought of infelicity in Devachan; both are
effects, not causes, and these effects are the results of the previous life.

Passing on from the condition of Devachan, comes the state of Nirvana, which is a "sublime state of conscious rest in omniscience." It is that perfect condition of the human soul in its preparatory state to the higher condition of pure spirit, or Atma, the highest condition known to the Buddhistic philosophy. The conditions of man, according to this conception, are divided into seven degrees or parts:

1 The body, or *Rupa*.
2 Vitality, or *Prana* or *Jiva*.
3 Astral, or *Linga Sharira*.
4 Animal soul, or *Karma Rupa*.
5 Human soul, or *Manas*.
6 Spiritual soul, or *Buddhi*.
7 Spirit, or *Atma*.

xx.

(7) "The Manas lighter than the damp, sluggish air."
Manas means the spirit.

(8) "Would leave the rupa and arise thro' the law of Karma."
The rupa is the body; the Karma, that attendant character, or aroma, of the soul that determines its state in the future.

AN HONEST PRAYER.

——:——

Oh! thou invisible power
  That moves the heart and stirs the brain.
Give sordid vice a transient hour
  And let within my bosom reign
A purer thought, a chaster love
Than aye within my bosom move.

No trust I place in gods unknown,
  To them I raise no gloomy fane;
The pregnant knee I bend to none:
  No priest I tithe, no sect I claim:
I worship 'neath no gilded dome,
But praise the good in man alone.

Oh! let me at his shrine adore
  The good that speaks through his address:
And let me love him more and more,
  Nor love the smiles of virtue less.
Nor do to others, bond or free,
That I would not have done to me.

Make me too great to do a wrong,
  Too weak to sin, too proud to lie.
Too rich to wear another's crown,
  Too poor to sport a coward's eye,
Too kind to start a tear to flow,
Too good to cause another woe.

Oh! give me strength of nerve and mind
  To earn through life the bread I eat.
Keep me in peace with all mankind:
  Let fraternal smiles my presence great:
Let no one say in life's great throng
That I have ever done him wrong.

Aid me to work a great reform
  Without the hope of fee or pelf.
Before I chide another's wrong,
  Teach me to first reform myself:
Learn to eschew the faults I own
And blight the seeds of passion sown.

Thou motive force within my brain,
  Let me invoke thee while I can.

Oh! let fraternal justice reign
  And man become the friend of man;
For he alone, of all the train,
  Can grace a savior's proud domain.

BOREAS.

Old Boreas comes with a scowl on his face,
  From the seas of the north and land of despair;
His coat is of snow, and his boots are of ice;
  Has frost for his whiskers; icicles for hair;
He whistles and whistles wherever he goes,
Not minding the weather, or caring for clothes.

He sweeps through the forest and over the glen,
  And spreads on the ground a white shroud as he goes
With manners so rude, that whenever he can,
  Through each little crevice, obtrudes he his nose,
And once he has ingress, audacious and bold,
He makes all about him feel chilly and cold.

A blast from his nostrils makes hoary the air,
  And freezes the waters of river and lake.
He nips with his teeth the green boughs until bare,
  And leaves devastation wide strewed in his wake:
Whatever he touches, with finger or breath,
Assumes at his bidding the visage of death.

He comes from the north with a rush and a roar;
  With a storm in his mouth, and blasts in his hand.
He raps at the window, and screams at the door;
  And shoots frigid arrows, like frost through the land—
With eyes of fierce frore, he pierces the throng,
And snaps at the ground as he passes along.

As an animal wild, unloosed from his cage,
  Flies hither and thither in search of his prey.
Incited by hunger, and goaded by rage,
  He bites every object that comes in his way;
And drinks up the water wherever 'tis found,
Then away and away he goes with a bound.

Mad, fierce and courageous, he howls through the plain
  And spreads freezing terror wherever he goes,
Nor slackens his speed, nor tightens his reins
  In the fiercest of gales, in rain storms or snows;

But in the cold frost-land his recluse is chosen
Where th' air is congealed and ocean is frozen.

But Notus, fair dame of the south, with her wiles,
   Comes conquering on like a float on the wing,
And flushes his face with the press of her smiles,
   And quiets his howl by the music of spring:
Disrobes him of terror by a whiff of her breath,
And gives him sweet life by a genial death.

SELFISHNESS.

This world is one vast battlefield,
   And mankind forms the armies;
Each one for self his weapon wield
   And there is where the harm is.

The fight begins when life begins,
   And all through life it rages;
And each with all the world contends—
   It's been thus through all ages.

Some strive for love and some for fame,
   Some for hate and some for pelf;
But each one through the love of gain,
   Contends with all the world for self.

Each act, each deed, each wish in life,
   The all of each man proves it;
Be it for peaceful meed or strife,
   Some selfish motive moves it.

The merchant feigns a blandish smile,
   And apes all modern graces,
And talks quite smooth that he might sell
   His shelf-worn goods and laces.

The doctor sells his potent pills,
   And tells of their great wonders;
But when, forsooth, his nostrum kills
   The grave conceals his blunders.

The lawyer wears an honest mien,
   And never slights a duty;
He first acquits the rogue, I ween,
   And then bears off the booty.

The parson bends the pregnant knee.
  And prays for saint and sinner;
But all the while, "Oh, God!" thinks he.
  Let me come out the winner."

And thus the world goes on and on,
  The all of each man proves it;
Be it for peaceful meed or song,
  Some selfish motive moves it.

THE GODS OF OLD.

Great gods! Look'd down from bending skies
  Through glowing eyes of sunlit stars:
The moon with sapient smiles arose
  To blend her sweetest grace with Mars.

In every breeze that listed by,
  The whispering of some god was heard:
In every cloud that flit the sky,
  An easy couch for him was spread.

In tones of thunder oft he spoke
  And lightning flash'd from out his eyes:
In zigzag skelp'd the mountain slope
  And fill'd with lurid flame, the skies.

He rode upon the ocean waves
  And ruled the raging storm with ease:
He plac'd the tints on matin rays
  And sweet perfum'd the roses' leaves.

A god o'erlook'd the battle-din
  And fill the winding stream with gore;
A god bent o'er the faithful slain
  And bore them to the peaceful shore.

A halo, round the mother's bed
  Who smil'd upon the infant born,
By god with loving will was spread,
  But oft, too oft, 'twas born to mourn.

A god control'd in things terene
  And reign'd eternal on a throne:
His potent powers remain'd unseen:
  His wishes taught, himself unknown.

He moved upon the vasty deep;
 Disrobed dead nature of its shroud :
Awoke the atomies from sleep;
 'Twas this! 'twas this, that man call'd god.

Those felt the most his secret test,
 Who knew the least of Nature's laws :
Those know the most of God's behest,
 Who know the least of natural cause.

THOMAS PAINE.

Thomas Paine, for his virtues, obtained the reproof
 Of dishonest tongues and the frowns
Of tyrants, because he stood steadfast for the truth,
 And worshiped its uttermost bounds.

He followed its trail 'cross the aqueous deep,
 Where tyranny erstwhile had rest;
Where Liberty lay as a giant asleep,
 On the rape of an innocent breast.

Paine wrote; the giant arose from his slumber.
 With all his powers assembled;
Impel'd by his mind of magical wonder
 Paine spoke; and tyranny trembled.

He arose with the mien of a cavalier brave,
 And cleft the deep air with his spear,
And swore that Columbia should not be the grave
 Of struggling liberty dear.

Tyranny, goaded to the verge of despair,
 Suffused every throne with his groans;
But swore, "Liberty's stench should batten the air.
 And bleach on the plains, his curs'd bones."

"Ah! Wis thou?" the tyrant, with irony said.
 "For ages in sleep you have lain."
" 'Tis true!" said Liberty, raising his head,
 "I 'woke through the magic of Paine."

"Fy!" lipped the tyrant, and sardonically smiled :
 "Your presumption is beyond measure;
Remember thou art but old England's child,
 And she can chastise thee at pleasure."

"I groaned, as a child, beneath Tyranny's ban."
  Liberty replied with disdain;
"But now I defy you, I grew to a man,
  Through the magical powers of Paine."

Reaching forth, he caught Johnny Bull by the cuff
-   And placed his foot on him amain
And said. "You shall feel," as he gave him a buff.
  "The magical powers of Paine."

TO MOLLIE.
—— : ——

I will within your album write.
  As others here have pen'd;
And on this spotless page indict
  The wishes of a friend.

I wish you all the joys of earth.
  That honest maids may gain;
I wish you many years of health.
  Without an ache, or pain.

I wish your future may be grand.
  And "times" not very hard:
I wish when you may give your hand.
  You'll get a clever *pard*.

I wish for him a pleasure, too,
  When both of you are old,
That he can say, come weal! come woe!!
  My *frow* would never scold.

I wish that you then, too, can say.
  My *pard* was always good:
He's fed me well; and day by day,
  Has cut my oven wood.

Now one thing more I will have pen'd.
  Then wind this wishing up,
That when it raineth soup, my friend.
  Your dish be right side up.

HYPATIA.

Hypatia, pure of heart, and learn'd was there.
    Esteem'd of virtue and of grace refined;
Whose eloquence of beauty, chaste and rare,
    Won Orestes; and to her cultured mind,
Cynesius bow'd a willing head; and
    Theon lived thro' his favor'd daughter's brain.
Whose luster shed an honor great and grand
    On Plutonius; but it was in vain.
For Cyril lived, who would her fame displace.
    And in piece meal tore her fragile frame,
And on Cœcarium wrote his own disgrace—
    Hypatia dead, but Cyril lives in shame.

WITTEN'S YEAST IS RISING.

To help a man out, by the name of Witten, who was the manufacturer of a hop yeast, I advanced him some money. Afterwards, without authority, he bought some articles of A. J. Fernigee. Not paying for them, Mr. Fernigee wrote that he would sue me, if I did not pay the bill.

You write to me,
    Dear Fernigee,
That you're going to sue:
    If that be so,
    You ought to know,
The step you'll surely rue.

First note the cost,
    And time, too, lost;
Make, too, a calculation;
    If you succeed,
    How much you'll bleed
In purse and botheration.

These legal fights,
    Cause wakeful nights,
And trouble through the day:
    You scarce begin
    The naughty thing,
Before you have to pay.

You'll find, dear sir,
    The officer,
Before he serves your writs.

Will hint to thee
To pay his fee,
Or you may look for fits.

And you will learn,
Quite soon, dear Fern.,
This is no empty dream;
The parties get
The curded milk;
The lawyers get the cream.

Why you should now
Kick up a row,
To me is quite surprising;
If you'll keep still,
You'll get your bill,
For Witten's yeast is rising.

THE MEASURE OF RIGHT.

"Please, sir, give me what you can,"
Of an aged and truthful man,
I asked: "and all you have, of light,
That guides the mind to what is right."
"Right, sir, is gaged, full well I know,
Against the cause of weakest foe.
On him the frown of contempt stays,
The arm of strength commands the bays.
The lauds aloud from out the world
Is poured upon the flag unfurl'd,
And laureates the victor's stand
The noble chief; the valiant band,
And execrate as sinful flows
The fell'd one's plea, his ruined cause:
For this is true, whate'er the cause,
Success is greeted with applause,
And most mankind with smiles contend,
To give Success a helping hand,
And with a bow, though dark the deeds,
Commend the stroke where Victory leads,
And with false servile smiles extend
The hand of welcome as a friend.
But what chagrin and woeful wail
Befall on those who start and fail?

A struggling soul, e'en on the strand
Can scarcely get a helping hand;
And when received, this fact suppress,
It comes from those too, in distress.

From springs of sorrow, kindness flows,
Affliction feels another's woes.
A tear will trinkle unrestrained
When Want perceives a fellow pained;
And Want would languish at the door
Did not the poor care for the poor.

READ THEIR FATE BETWEEN THE LINES.

We are living, we are acting
  In a grand and glorious time,
And the ages we are moulding
  Will bring their ultimates sublime.

We are reaping from the ages,
  Reaching back to long ago;
We are reading from the pages,
  Wrote in words of human woe.

Pages that portray the actions
  Of the ruling spirits then;
Of the grim tumultuous factions,
  And the crimes of many men.

Of the wars and revolutions,
  Failures and successes grand:
Of contentions and commotions
  That for aye have filled the land.

But there is a sadder reading,
  Of those dark and gloomy times:
Which is worthy of our heeding;
  'Tis read between the written lines.

'Tis the reading of the anguish
  Wrung from bleeding hearts and sad:
Hearts that grieve unknown and languish.
  With the living and the dead.

'Tis the anguish of the lone one,
  'Tis the wailing of the weak.

It is the patient, helpless throng
  That of their wrong, never speak.

Those that struggle on in sorrow
  With no other hope in view;
Moil to-day and mourn to-morrow;
  'Tis the millions for the few.

It is the millions for the few,
  'Twas the same in ancient times:
Which facts are veil'd from public view:
  Are only read between the lines.

We are living, we are acting,
  In an age and at a time,
And if we are up and doing
  We can make our lives sublime.

We can change the wheel of power
  And its weight on these dark times:
We can make Oppression cower,
  And read his fate between the lines.

THE SPRITE OF GLEN BOKEN.

——:——

Near the old Glen Boken, at the break of the sea,
  Where the billows are dashed to death on the stones,
A dense, shaggy woodland stands back from the lea
  And frowns in grim visage at th' half-covered bones
That lay in its breaks, all decaying and bare,
Like dread leaves in the book of human despair.

One eventide gloomy, in a half frighten'd tread,
  Enhanced by the moans in the trees of Glen Boken,
I thought as I went of the wails of the dead;
  The glare of their eyes and appeals last spok'n,
When Gnoman, the pirate, chose this as the wold
Of his victims, that perished through his greed for gold.

I thought of the manes that in darkness here strom'd,
  Half muffled in shadows all gloomy in gore—
I thought of the spirits returning that own'd
  The blood that enriched here the earth, long before.
My hair commenced rising and my flesh creeping,
It seemed to me plainly a spectre was speaking

From each craggy tree top. My pick and my spade,
  Companions most dear to my heart, in this stream,
Fell from my trembling hands and on th' ground laid.
  Then I wished, how I wished, I was not alone
In this gloomy woodland where the hoot of great owls,
Kept echoing back the refrain of grim ghouls.

I thought of legends told by denizens old,
  Near the breaks and fell of yawning Glen Boken.
'Twas said that the pirate secreted his gold,
  Th' seal of whose secret had never been broken
Except by the legends of old people told,
That hard by Glen Boken he'd buried his gold.

My arm felt ren *ved and I grabbed for my spade,
  For I knew, well I knew, from legends quite old,
That Gnoman, the pirate, had here about laid
  The guilt of his calling, his crime-gotten gold.
"I'd give half the gains," I convulsively thought,
"If I could find a seer to point out the spot."

Yet I was confirmed, with my pick and my spade,
  Now tight in my hands held, both restive and bold.

That before the night waned, with my burnished blade
  I'd be breaking the lock of that chest of gold;
And soon I could strut with my coffers well fill'd,
But refrained from the thought of the groans of the kill'd.

Th' possessor of that which I wished to possess,
  I knew for his crimes I was not in th' blame,
But felt half inclined to kneel down and confess,
  That the jingle of gold drowns th' feelings of shame
And honors the brow, though with guilt thickly spread.
By wronging the living and robbing the dead.

While thus I was thinking—half speaking alone,
  In that gloom hanging woodland of Glen Boken,
Where the moon never smiled and the sun never shone
  In that shadow of shadows, this was spoken
And plainly, quite plainly, it fell on my ear
As if it was uttered by some knowing seer:

"I'll point you the spot where the treasure is hid,
  But first, a word I will give you of warning;
I warn you to note it, and heed it," he said.
  "Take what you will, but depart before morning,
For if you are found here, in th' morn's early bloom
You'll feel the full wage of a wizard's deep gloom."

Whose smile is ecstatic, but follows his frowns,
  The pall of remorse and the trail of distress.
This fell is his reign. Here his shadow abounds.
  His wish is his will, and here Cimmerius
Obeys and blights with his look whoe'er is found
At th' breaking of light in this ghoul-haunted ground.

"I swear by my soul, dearest guard." I replied.
  "To leave here ere morning, if I but behold
The spot where old Gnoman did actually hide,
  From the ken of the world, his treasures of gold."
"Then come," he said, in a sepulchral tone,
"But tread not upon a skull, or a bone."

"Come, I will conduct you 'mid shadow and gloom,
  To the spot, very spot, where Gnoman of old
Secreted his spoils; where he buried the boon
  Of his crimes. But beware, for many I've told
Where Gnoman, the pirate, had buried his gold,
But all disregarded what you I have told."

"Like millions of others, entrammel'd by greed,
　Forget the prime lessons of life, often told,
And embarrass themselves with wrongs, ere they heed
　The warning of risking too much for bright gold.
Beware of the shades and the mantle of night,
Their shrouds are dissolved by the glow of the light."

Over the cliffs of rocks and down through the glen,
　I followed my chaperone with pick and spade
To a darker dark place, forbidding, and then
　He halted, and in a coarse whisper he said:
"This is the spot that environs his sins
And this is the hour that sorrow begins."

I took up my pick, and with might, and with main.
　I cleft the tough sward that thick around laid;
I severed its bosom and rootlets in twain
　And then with skill deftly, I took up my spade,
And the second deep delve to my utter surprise
I struck the old chest containing the prize.

As quick as old Niffin, I bursted the lock;
　Threw the lid open wide, and lo! and behold
Lay millions before me. Imagine my shock!
　If the inmates of hell had taken the wold,
A more hideous laugh and demon-like scream,
Would not have my poor soul pierced keener. I ween

A more frightful noise was before never heard.
　Those shaggy old tree tops, and tangled vine bows
Were adorned with delvers for gold, by a word
　From the wizard spoken, and now to arouse
Me again said: "Metamorphosed like they
Are, will you be, if found here at break of day."

"I thank you, my friend, for your caution so queer,
　I feel in no peril of being like they;
I'll gather my gold ere the sun's rays appear
　And away I will go to my home by the sea."
"Ha! ha!! ha!!! they all think that," he said, and smiled.
"Hark at their song, now, so weird and wild."

　　　Gold! gold!! glittering gold!!!
　　Under the grassroots and under the mould,
　　It brings more distress to millions, we're told,
　　Than poverty's wage on the young and the old.
　　　Gold! gold!! glittering gold!!!
　　Under the grass roots and under the mould."

"Delve, delve, devil's work done,
From the shades of night to the break of the sun:
Thus have our courses for ages been run,
Always are delving, but never get done;
  Delve, delve, devil's work done
From the shades of night to the break of the sun."

"Of gold, I've enough," I said. "I will go now,
  But going, I leave here a sigh of regret.
I can buy me a home, a pig and a cow,
  My wife a new gown, my daughter a jacket.
With this I can get all the comforts of life,
  And live like a prince with my daughter and wife.

How temping it looks! Must I go quite so soon?
  I'll take one more eagle, 'twill come in good play:
It lies there so useless: that shining doubloon
  Seems tempting, I may need that some future day.
Now, while I'm providing for declining days
I'll provide me to ride to church in a chaise.

With my ruffles all starched and my hair in a queue
  I'll go riding along like a lord in his pride:
I'll batten the parson, I'll rent me a pew;
  My child, winsome lass, on a palfry shall ride:
Like quality folks we will revel in wine:
We'll rise about ten, and at six o'clock, dine.

I'll play at the cards and throw tricky dices:
  Will win the esteem of the rich and the grand
By learning their manners and aping their vices:
  I'll sport velvet fingers and glove-incased hand:
I'll dress in neat fashion from tip to the toe,
And always in circles the best I will go.

Ah! that demoniacal yell, half laugh, half scream,
  Shocks every nerve and is wrecking my brain:
Those delving old miners are laughing, I ween,
  At my speculations: but ah! they again
Are turned to grim spectres, a horrible sight.
"Yes," whispered the wizard, "the morn's early light."

Ah! the morn's shooting gray is streaking the sky,
  And I must away, my work is complete.
Where is my gold? It has disappeared, and I
  Am bewildered and witched, and my very feet

Are grown to the turf and myself to a tree.
And all the years hence my moaning shall be

Gold! gold!! glittering gold!,!!
Has caused more anguish than ever was told:
Delusive to youth, deceptive to old,
A snare to the weak, a bait for the bold.
Gold! gold!! glittering gold!!!
Has caused more anguish than ever was told.

THE INFINITUDES.

—:——

ETERNITY.

Oh ! thou eternity, in vain
    I strive to fathom thee;
Could I count the sands, grain by grain,
    That gird the mighty sea,
A thousand years might roll between,
    Each number of a sand,
Which under grand old ocean gleam
    And glisten in the strand.
Then could I take them one by one,
    And bear them from the sea,
One moment will not have begun—
    Such is eternity.

MATTER.

Oh ! thou omnipotent
And omnipresent
    Infinitude, Matter,
    Thee we adore.
Thy modes of expressions,
And infinitude after
Infinitude of manifestations,
    And thy power
    Are inexpressible
    And incomprehensible.
Thou art the one great all that is,
    Was, or ever can be;
You hold the two eternities,
    Oh! thou ubiquity;
Thy arms reach out from sphere to sphere:
Thy bosom vast all force contains;
Thou art the sum of ev'rywhere,
Of life and soul and all the things
    Within the universe, or out,
    Formed and unformed, and phas'd thou art
Into the infinitesimal;
The beautiful of the beautiful.
Thou art the one great, grand
Consummation of the grand
Whole.   The substance and substratum
Of ev'ry sphere and ev'ry atom;
Thou art the one without beginning,

Indestructible, without ending;
   Thou the visible
   And invisible
    Of all things,
By thyself brought forth.
   We know springs
From thy omniscient worth.
Every entity and birth.

Ring thy praise on every ear,
   To every eye thy grandeur gleams:
Thy throne is the eternal sphere
   Of space: thy life the omniscient dreams
    Of time,
    And thine,
Is the unrivaled power,
   Kingdom, glory, forever.

SPACE.

A thought might span a thousand lives.
   Like bounding to the sun.
Then on! fly on, while Time survives.
   Yet Space lies farther on.

Could lightning stride the universe
   Like twinkling of an eye,
It could not, during time, traverse
   The space beyond the sky.

Could man cement a thousand minds,
   A thousand thoughts in one,
He could not reach its vast confines,
   That space beyond the sun.

Fly on as light flies in its speed,
   Or sight glimpse in its train,
Till seas shall take the mountain's stead
   And ocean fill the plain.

Fly while the sun in splendor glows,
   The stars in beauty shine:
Fly while the tide of ocean flows,
   The moon her course incline.

Fly till the earth shall be no more,
   Till Time shall cease its race:
Lies thy expanse still on before.
   The vast domain of space.

OUR MOTHER HAS LEFT US.

——:——

On coming home from the Watkins Glen Freethinkers' convention, full of hopes, and happy in the expectation of realizing, at no distant day, man, as brother to brother bound. Revolving in our minds the pleasing incidents of the convention and renewing in our hearts the pleasant and esteemed acquaintances there formed, with a desire to meet them on many like occasions and renew the bonds of friendship and good will. But alas! that flow of joy and fervent heart glow of pleasure was transformed into the deepest grief by being struck with the sad news of the death of our wife's mother, Elizabeth Cunningham, of Joplin, Mo., who died August 22nd, 1882. She had been sick for several months, but we thought she was getting better and would soon be restored to health. That thought proved a delusion, and good old mother passed to the call of nature and left a void in the circle that can never be filled again. What a blow it was to the buoyant heart of our wife. She was not prepared for such sad news, and it fell like a pall on her spirits.

Our good mother was sixty-five years old. She was devoted to her children and family. She is entitled to the highest encomium that can be placed on any woman : which is, she was a true mother.

She was laid away by the side of her son, Winfield P. Cunningham, in the Carthage cemetery, where she rests in peace ; beloved by all who knew her, and reverenced with lasting affection by her family.

We can but imagine we see her sweetly, quietly sleeping, and in our heart must say :

Fold her hands gently
  Across her calm breast,
Close her eyes tenderly,
  In peace let her rest.

Smooth down her silken locks,
  Adjust them with care—
How calm and sweet she looks,
  How pure, and yet fair.

Wipe her face carefully,
  In love bathe her brow,
Care for her lovingly,
  Attentively now.

Arrange a rose neatly,
  To smile on her breast,
Portraying so sweetly
  Her Eden of rest.

A gift from Rosary
  Should garland her bier :
As dew on each flower
  Should glisten a tear.

Take her up gently,
　With sorrow profound:
Bear her off easily
　And lisp not a sound.

Let her down carefully,
　Easily and kind;
Turn not sorrowfully,
　To leave her behind.

Now cover her neatly,
　Exchange not a word,
That she may sleep sweetly
　Beneath the green sward.

It should not now grieve us
　To go away home,
She does not now need us,
　She is not alone.

The angels will guard her,
　Birds merrily sing,
The flowers that wither
　Returneth each Spring.

She, like the bright flowers
　That wither and die,
Will smile again ours
　In the sweet "by and by."

Turn from the sepulchre,
　She resteth there well.
Bid a by-bye to her,
　But say not farewell.

RATIONAL THANKSGIVING.

—:—

I

Our national chief has ordered this day
Set apart from our daily vocations.
We're ordered to thank, give praise and to pray
To the Lord for his kind applications
Of manifold blessings untold.
The rich render thanks for a plethoric purse,
The well, for their health and vigor of frame;
The poor may thank God, that things are no worse,
The sick may thank him for not having more pain
Than their feeble bodies can hold.

II.

The preachers thank God and claim that He willed
Turkeys well fatted and chickens all dressed;
Houses neat furnished and larders well filled
With luxuries of life, for money possessed
And other things had for mere asking.
He's thanked for our laws and wealth of our nation,
For bountiful crops and peace through the land,
For Independence He's paid adoration—
Our freedom, it is said, came by his command,
And all other things by his tasking.

III.

If preachers for chickens to God are indebted,
If He's the provider of what they admire,
Who should the chickens thank for being beheaded?
Who should the turkeys thank for not roosting higher,
And saving themselves from the pot?
If God gave us peace and plenty of mammon,
And gladdened our hearts with provisions in store:
Who should the thousands thank dying from famine?
Who should the nations thank bleeding from war?
Or a soldier wounded by shot?

IV.

If the rich should thank God because they're not poor,
For their gold in the bank and government bonds:
For ships on the sea and railroads on shore,
For great lowing herds and rich fertile lands,
With a life of pleasure and ease;
Who should the poor thank for poverty's wage:
For hollow-eyed Want, that stands at the door:
For hunger and rags and homeless old age;

For the kicks and cuffs that fall to the poor,
   And other sweet morsels like these?

v.

Who should we thank for the wars of the crusades,
   For the blood that was spilled, for the lives that they cost,
For the woe that marked the dreary dark ages,
   When learning was banished and the sciences lost,
     And their votaries hunted like beasts:
Who should we thank for the Lord's long sable reign,
   When witches were burned and heretics slaughtered:
When the sky was begrimed with fagot and flame;
   When infants were murdered and mothers were quartered,
     To hallow the church of the priests?

vi.

If God gives us health and vigor of frame,
   Making us hearty, hale, active and strong,
Who sends our distresses, sickness and pain,
   And burdens the millions struggling on,
     Contending with fate and diseases?
Who should the deformed, the crippled from birth,
   The sickly, the blind, halt, helpless and lame,
Praise for their ailments and crosses of earth?
   If God controls all things, who should they blame
     For sending those ills when he pleases?

vii.

If God commands plenty and pleasure at will,
   And holds all the good things of life in his hand,
Who brings the scourges, all pestilence and ill
   Luck to the people, throughout the broad land,
     To vex us and curse us through life?
Why force on a being our homage and praise,
   For sending more evil to mankind than good:
For sending the curses of war and disease,
   Earthquakes and storms, cyclones, fire and flood,
     Seasoned with crime, bloodshed and strife?

viii.

A mother must thank God for her prattling babe,
   For the pleasure and joy it brings to her heart:
Then thank him again when its dear form is laid
   In the cold chilly ground and she must depart,
     With her heart in the grave buried there.
Who should we thank when death comes to the door,
   And takes from the circle our loveliest bloom,

And bears it away to be with us no more,
  And renders its memory our saddest gloom,
  And its death an infliction severe.

IX.

We could thank with more grace if God would but turn
  His business affairs into more even channels;
If he'd equalize things and give more concern
  To the wails of distress, and less to the trammels
    That curse the whole human race.
If he would but change his manner of doing,
  Make pleasure the rule and not the exception
To life; render us happy and not be sowing
  The seeds of sorrow, woe, strife and contention,
    To bring us down to disgrace.

X.

"Render to Cæsar the things which are Cæsar's,
  And to the Lord which belong to the Lord,"
Is a rule of his own, and very well pleases
  My sense of duty, and ought to accord
    With the author's conception of right.
Then should we e'er meet in the world yet to come,
  I'll risk my whole case on the rule he made here,
And render to Cæsar that which is his own,
  Although it deprives the good Lord over there
    Of thanks from my heart here to-night.

XI.

Who should we thank for the flag that waves o'er us,
  For the glow of its stripes and its glittering stars;
Who bore it aloft in conflicts before us,
  Who brought to us victory in all of our wars;
    Was it God? No. But our fathers.
Who spilled their blood in Old Revolution,
  And left their bones bleaching on many a field;
Who laid down their lives with patriot's devotion,
  And sank in the conflict rather than yield.
    Was it God, or our forefathers?

XII.

Who severed the chains that bound us as slaves?
  Who gave us our rights as a nation of freemen?
Whose weatherbeat bones lie in unknown graves,
  That we have the rights of freemen and women,
    Was it God? I answer no.
Who sent her last son to the battles' fierce brawl,
  Who kissed his fair cheek and bade him to go

To return to her, only when tyranny's pall
  Should cover the form of our country's last foe?
    Was it God?   A thousand times no.

XIII.

Whose bones dot the sun-scorched fields of the South?
  Who met the foe when rebellion had risen?
Who read his own death in the cannon's dark mouth?
  Who was it that famished in Anderson prison?
    Was it God?   My heart responds no.
Who struck the fetters from three million slaves?
  Who saved this nation in tact, as a whole?
Who rightly deserves our devotion and praise?
  Whose name shall be written on Honor's bright scroll?
    Is it God's?   The world should say no.

XIV.

Who furrows the face of the deep raging sea,
  And sails every ocean, around and around?
Who causes our flag to float easy and free
  In every part of the world to be found?
    Is it God?   You know it is not.
Then let us not thank him for what he's not done.
  Nor force our obeisance upon him again;
'Tis better his name remain ever unsung,
  Than those be forgotten who made us freemen
    And gave us the land we have got.

A SONG TO BACCHUS.

——:——

Let those who wish to please by prayer,
    Invoke the god which suits them;
But we can please the Bacchian ear
    The best by song or anthem.

This patron god smiles on the vine
    And loads its pendent tresses,
With grapes that make the ruby wine
    That sparkles in our glasses.

CHORUS.

Then pour us some wine,
    The soul of the vine,
It makes our nerves tingle, each quaff;
    It first will beguile
    Our lips to a smile,
And then we break out with a laugh.
    Ha! ha!! ha!!! ha! ha!! ha!!!
    It makes us feel fine
    When jolly good wine,
Goes dancing through our veins, ha! ha!!

I envy not the epicure,
    Nor will the judgment flatter,
Of him who feels himself secure
    By filling up on water.

Cold water is a useful thing
    Like all things else, I'm thinking?
'Twill do to float great vessels in,
    But will not do for drinking.

CHORUS.

A LAWYER'S STORY.

——:——

The lawyers are
Proverbial for
Their stories quaint and pithy;
They often run
To doubtful fun,
But sometimes are quite witty.

One day they sat
In chit, chit, chat
On subjects dry and old;
Until one spoke,
Let's have a joke!
Squiggs has a new 'n, I'm told.

Squiggs, out with one,
Let's have some fun!
The world rolls easy by,
Squiggs very droll,
Said, " 'Pon my soul
I never tell a lie."

"If you don't choke
On that huge joke,
A lie is not worth telling,"
Tom Jones replied,
Then drolly sighed,
And set the tother yelling.

"My native pride,"
Squiggs then replied;
"Precludes my story telling;
I'll break the rule,
If you'l be cool,
And stop that 'fernal yelling.

But I forsooth
Must tell the truth,
I can't do otherwise;
If that won't do
To amuse you,
Friend Jones will tell you lies.

One night last June
Bright was the moon,

I heard a chant of groans;
I knew in fine
The cause was wine—
Sit still, don't blush so Jones.

Poor fellow tugg'd
And pull'd and hugg'd,
To keep a post from falling;"—
"Now drat your bones!"
Exclaimed poor Jones,
"That's a whopper you're telling."

THE SPHYNX.

It makes us sad. It brings a sigh,
To see an old religion die.
Like some great leviathan strong,
It wreathes, struggles, holds out long
    Against the inevitable,
    The law is irrevocable;
"That which had a beginning
Must also have an ending."
The gods we love, adore, admire,
Must find, at last, a funeral pyre.
E'en those, who now are most ador'd
Will in time become ignored.
Like all the myths of ages cast
Be relegated to the past,
And other fancies, other themes
Engross the mind with other dreams.

The future will attune its lays
To sing of our benighted ways,
As we can speak in thunder tones
Of ucas from those sculptured stones,
When Thebes smiled on a fertile plain
And flourish'd through the thousands slain,
Who worship'd twixt the Sphynx's paws
And paid obeisance to its laws,
Which from its stone mind came evolved
'Till Œdipus brought the riddle solved.

Now in a bed of unwash'd sands,*
    In silence and in solitude
Its cold, black form in wonder blends

Its weakness with its magnitude.

Three thousand years have come and gone,
  Three thousand circles sank to rest,
Since Thebans raised a sacred song
  To please this monster's stolid breast.

This god is dead, the lichen deigns
  Not to adorn his begrim'd form;
No ivy mantles his remains,
  Or grass around his bier is grown.

Amphion, by his tuneful lyre†
  Reared the city's lofty head;
Now silence marks its funeral pyre
  For we are told its god is dead.

*The Sphynx now marking the site of ancient Thebes, is heaped around
by sand that is absolutely barren of all kinds of vegetation.

†It was a tradition among the Thebans that Amphion built the walls of
their city by the sound of his lyre.

THE EARTH.

Oh! beautiful, beautiful earth!
  Rivers long and oceans wide and deep,
  Silver lakes and air of mighty sweep,
Allow my thoughts reverent birth.
  Awake my heart again from sleep
And lift my sluggish mind from the throw
Of gloom, that I may see and know
  Thy fullness and grandeur complete.

Oh! let me drink thy flowing beauty in;
Ken clouds upon their aqueous wing:
And all of nature's bounteous weal.
Oh! let me appreciate and feel.

Bright morning fair, dew-dress'd and cool,
Be a teacher to me. Thy school
Of loveliness will grace impart,
Add meekness to a willing heart.
Subdue my mind to thy control,
Awake the windows of my soul
To see the glowing sun at noon
  And stars that get the sky above,
That twinkle at the swimming moon
  Discoursing symphonies of love.

On the new life-bud of swelling spring,
  Flush on the cheek of Nature fair,
Latonia flits a balmy wing
  And prints her kisses, rich and rare.
That bursts into the summer bloom
  And ripens into autumn sear,
Reminders that the turn of noon
  Typifies man's short journey here.

Oh! parent of our present bourn,
  Bend on me thy enchanting face,
And drive from me the frown ill-born,
  And plant within my bosom grace,
That I may see thee as thou art;
The all of good, the ev'ry part;
The all there is of Heaven's store;
The now, the was, the evermore.

Oh! beautiful, beautiful earth!

The grave of all, our life, our birth.
To the mind unwed to guile
The earth presents a living smile;
'Tis seen in all of nature sweet,
The bending sky, the ocean deep,
The brook that murmurs at the feet;
The balmy air, the tuneful birds;
The lambkins gay, the lowing herds,
And all the world, with joys prolong
The measures of its rhythmic song.

Where can man, in his dreams afar,
Find greater field for bliss than here?
Oh! earth I love thee! I adore
Thy completeness; I love thee, the more
I know of thee and thy rich store.

Oh! thou art full of lovely things;
    From each atom rightly known
And appreciated, there springs
    An interesting beauty, shown
Through its life. A rich treasure
To the mind, a glorious pleasure
Meeting every want of the soul;
Every demand in the control
Of our nature, finds solace here,—
Use and beauty reign everywhere.

Nature vast in its casualties
Has produced more realities
Than the dreamer of dreams can find
Within his sleepy, rambling mind,
In its wildest fancies. The eyes
Ken beauties all around. The skies,
The earth, the air, the ocean deep
And tiny grass have tongues that speak,
And tell of latent beauties hidden
In the womb of Time. Forbidden
To the dull, dead mind,
That can only find
Pleasure through the appetite,
And joy in the sable night
Of man's austere ignorance,
That now admits of no defense.

The rock-ribbed mountains speak to us

In tones grandiloquent. The rill
That trinkles down their aged sides
Join their symphonies, that sweetly fill
The heart with love, as downward glides
The limpid waters to vales below,
Where they may join the onward flow
Of the slow-moving placid stream,
As away to the ocean main
It flows, and where at last
Is swallowed up and lost
In its own immensity!
Oh! what intensity
Of thought and admiration thrills
Our very soul to view great hills,
Whose vine-clad brows with grace arise
To rift the curtains of the skies.

Beauty's fondest dreams of the sward
And dew-kissed flowers, still afford
The sweetest pleasure as they send
Their fragrance on the breeze, to blend
Their lovely smiles with whispering morn,
And dally on the new joys borne
By sun-lit rays of gleaming light,
As they paint on the skirts of night
The rosy tint of day unshent
By sable folds of darkness spent.
The sublimity of the flash
    Of lightning, around the mountain
Brow, playing, as the heavy crash
    Of thunder breaks on the fountain
Of nerve centres, as it bounds
    From side to side, from crest to crest,
Sending back echoes in its rounds,
    Falling fainter and fainter, till lost
In the dim, distant murmurings
Of the far wide plains' surroundings:
Find only their like in the inspired
    Grandeur, fearful to despair,
Of a raging sea storm, stirred
    With a mad and furious air;
Wrought to boiling gnarls, as it wreathes
To burst its rock confines, and breathes
A painful, mingling, distressing roar,

As it clashes and lashes the shore
In its terrible fury.   Deep
Running waves and surges sweep
The ocean bed.   Mists ascending
The while, with lightning's blare blending,
And lending new terror, to the scene.
  But when the storm winds lull,
  And the swift sea gull
Disports above the waves serene,
And the sun laps its golden rays
On the rolling, silvery sea waves,
As they subside to a peaceful calm,
The well trained mind in pure rapture then
Drinks in a new refreshing zest,
And thinks this, of all the worlds, the best.

The real of the earth is more wonderful,
And its unfoldments more beautiful
To the true child of thought
Than Conception ever wrought,
Or Fancy can portray.
Yes! It bears the soul away
To the realms of ecstatic bliss,
  As the unclouded mind goes out
To where the sky and ocean kiss,
  And silver wavelets play about
The laughing moonbeams of nightfall.

  How the swelling heart, brimming full
Of sweet emotions, thrills the nerves !
When the eye of beauty first observes
The fairest gleams of morning, sending
  Like golden ribbons up the sky ;
Its flushes pure, and freshly blending
With Night's dark curtain, spread across
The surface of the star-lit dorse,
To let the king of Day pass by.

Yes, smiling earth and starlit skies
Contain glorious mysteries
For man to investigate,
And, if of use, appropriate
To his own desires and needs;
For nature smiles where knowledge leads
And knowledge leads to pleasure—

In nature lies the treasure.
Oh, glorious, sweet necessity !
Let us love, praise and honor thee,
The one bright jewel in nature's course,
The resultant of dynamic force !
Our Home, our Earth and our heaven,
Most beautiful, beautiful heaven.

Oh ! judge me not a sinner blind;
    With heart seduced to evil ways;
Till you unfold unto my mind
    A fairer world than this to praise.

THE RAINBOW.

When the far western sky is red,
    We often turn the eye,
And ken the rainbow deftly spread
    Across the eastern sky
To trace it where its grandeur blends
With azure at the dipping ends;
Where we, in youthful years, were told,
Were always found full sacks of gold,
Which we could have to sport and spend
If we could reach the dipping end.

Delusive hope and painful fears
    Alternate cross'd our anxious brow,
Like visions of the later years
    That oft, too oft, deceive us, now.

THE BUTTERFLY.

Charming insect! Thou pretty thing !
Velvet body and silken wing !
Enchantment of a transient hour,
Flitting from flower to flower—
Gay butterfly, beautiful thing,
Who sips the purest nectar in.
Distill'd in starlight solitude,
In floral cells to be thy food.

Companion of my sweetest thought
Sport of the soul in heaven fraught,
Where Innocence on sylphan wing,
May flit like thee, thou pretty thing,
In beatitudes of pleasure,
And sip of heaven's pure measure.

Come fold thy wings, bewitching Fay,
On the verge of some flower gay
Rest for awhile thy tiny feet,
A perch design'd, by nature mete,
For thee to sit; gay butterfly,
Companion of the fairest eye.

Teach me to think, to ponder well,
Why thee through a dark cocoon cell
Up from invertebrates evolv'd,
And to a higher state install'd,
Unless it be that you thus teach,
Man has a higher sphere to reach.

THE MOON.

Sail on fair queen through the ether,
  Plow deep the cerulean sea;
Thy robes sweep the face of the heather,
  Thy smiles are of heaven to me.

On silver-tipped pinions of light,
  Through the diamond-deck'd field of the sky,
Queen, peerless sail on through the night,
  Sail on, thou sweet charm of the eye.

Fair passenger, sheen of the deep,
  Whose smiles bless the earth and the sea;
Whose visne is the boundless sweep;
  Oh! have you a smile left for me?

Thou empyrean queen of above;
  Fair charm of the stellar abyss!
Oh! seal the true passion of love,
  By impressing my lips with a kiss.

A GIRL OF NATURE.

I see with delight,
  A nature's true girl,
With cheeks like roses
  And natural curl.

With eyes of laughter,
  Enliv'ning her face,
Mirthfulness racing
  In innocent grace;

With never a sorrow,
  Her brow has defaced;
And never a stay
  Incumbered her waist.

With Nature's own rules
  Observed as her wealth,
The price of her wits
  Will bring years of health,

THE FIRST COO.

How often I have thought,
  When slyly I've eyed
A mother's eyes bending
  On baby, sweet pride
Of her heart, that heaven
  Has fruited complete,
When mother is patting
  Its two little feet.

Oh! what ecstacies run
  Her heart through and through,
When her fond ear catches
  Her darling's first coo.

MORN.

When the first gray streak of early
Morn, flashes through the deep, burly
Murk of night; and chases it away
To its sable vaults, before the day
God, smiling, comes to spread his flush
Of vermilion hue, with matin blush,
Across the bending sky; the pen
Or tongue, fails to paint his beauty then.

BIRDS.

Oh! for the gift of pen or words,
To paint the notes of cheerful birds
Sweet ton'd, as their warbling trills,
Softly thro' the heart, and fills
One's hungry soul with rapture;
Oh! how their intones capture
    The every thought,
    And how inwrought
In the heart, are the beautiful
Songs, so rich and so wonderful
On the balmy air floating,
    In a sweet and tuneful roll,
    To the intones of the soul,
As their joyful throats are noting
    Pleasures to the heart,
    That never will depart.

WHERE IS HEAVEN.

——:——

Where is heaven, with its bliss serene?
Is it beyond the things terene?
Does it surround a spacious throne
Which Deity esteems his own?
Has it a visne celestial,
Where none but sin-cleans'd spirits dwell?
Asked once an earnest-minded youth,
Whose greatest wish was further truth.

A voice from out the ether said:
"Heaven is where Love laughs with joy: speaks
From the eyes: lingers on the lips:
Blooms on the face; fruits on the head:
Lives in the heart; dances on the cheeks,
And gilds the throne where Mercy sits.

Heaven is where the eye imparts
The glow of joy, peace, friendship, mirth:
Where Concord, through confiding hearts,
Sends seeds of kindness to the earth,
And dries the tears of sorrow
From the eyes to-day, to-morrow.

Heaven, I have seen, typified
In the family of love.   By the side
Of a small rill, a vine-clad cot
Of a peasant is.   Wealth is not
In goods, but there stands
A contented man, in whose hands
The guerdon of the day is brought
For family meed; and in that cot
A frugal meal is spread,
And wife and children sped
With kisses on their lips, of love
For husband, father, friend, whose love
Goes out to meet and to greet them,
As they come to welcome and to meet him.
There is heaven.
There is heaven.
It is home, sweet and quiet home,
Which the family calls their own.
Here is heaven! yes, heaven sweet!
Heaven realized and complete.

THE SUNSET OF LIFE.

——:——

I wonder, often wonder, who
  Can remain unmoved with feelings
    Of grand emotion at even
Tide, as the old sun sets aglow
The placid bosom of the west,
  And smiling, sends his golden greeting
    To the outspread wings of heaven,
Then sinking calmly down to rest,
Whispers softly, sweetly and low,
      Good night,
        Fair world,
        Fair world,
      Good night;
I'll come again to-morrow.

I saw that old sun die last night
  In his golden lustre of age,
And slowly sinking out of sight,
  He spread upon the vermiel page
    Of heaven a smile
Of exquisite grace and richness.
    I watched him awhile,
  As he spead his tinted dye,
And gave the last strokes, with aerial brush,
  On the canvas of the sky;
Then fading, fading away to blend,
  Into star life, chaste, pure and bright—
Impressed me of that sweeter end,
  Sublimer look, last good night,
Loving smile, cheerful words and departing breath.
  Of silver Age sinking, sinking into death.
      "Good night,
        Dear friends,
        Dear friends,
      Good night;
We'll meet again to-morrow."

PHANTASMAGORIA OF THE GODS.

PREFACE.

The people generally, investigate all subjects brought to their notice, with their best abilities, and are governed by their mature judgment, except in matters of religion, which they take for granted. To doubt is rebellion; to falter is sin. They claim a kind of copyright on religion. With a double back-acting power as incident to the cause, it protects them from infringements and punishes the presumptuous, who may be inconsiderate enough to question what is taught in that respect; and it is considered a duty for the believers to suppress all disbelievers. If it cannot be accomplished by persuasion it is done by social ostracism, misrepresentation, slander and force, often resulting in the loss of property, liberty and life. It takes a brave person to brook the current of popular belief. The disbeliever is held up by the managers of religion as execrable—a bane to good society, with whom it is wrong to have social commerce.

This cramping of the human intellect has its effects, but yet it does not stop the workings of the mind, or prevent honest investigations into the truths and facts of all religious subjects, and into all questions pertaining to the supernatural.

We are told that there is but one true God. With that idea in view, we look back to the dawn of creation, when we are told man came fresh from the hand of the Creator, and we find the people in those days worshiping the cat, ibis, bull, crocodile, onions and leeks, as gods. The sun, moon and stars have all held the office of gods. If you will go out and investigate the claims of gods upon the people, you will be amazed at the pretentions, and bewildered at the numbers.

Go to Egypt, and you will find they have worshipped as gods, Neph, Amunor, Ammon, Pthab, Khem, Sati, Neith, Maut, Bubastis, Ra, Seb, Nupti, Osiris, Isis, Typhon, Horus, Apis, Serapis, Thoth, Anubus, Anaoke, Khunsu, Pecht, Athor, Cerberus and Sphinx.

Go to China, and we must not question, Toti, Pin-Tseuh, Kwan-Tan, Wan-Chank, Kwan-Ti, Chang-Ti, Fo, Omi-to, Gosh, Hwa-Kwang.

The Norsemen come to you with their Odin, Thor, Balder, Hermod, Tyr, Heimdal, Indun, Forsette, Jord, Frigg, Rind, Freyja, Frey, Gerd, Vider, Vale, Hoder, Gefjun, Sif, Uller, Eir, Ran, Loke, Hel, Jotuns.

The Persians had: Baal, Astarte, Ormuzd, Mithra, Ahriman.

The Brahmanic gods are, Brahma, Vishnu, Siva, Rama, Christna, Buddha, Juggernaut.

The Hindoo gods are, Indra, Varuna, Agni, Mitra, Prithivi, Soma, Maruts, Dawn, Yama.

Gods of the Semitic races: Baal, Ashtarath, Asshur, Moloch, Moladah, Melkart, Chemosh, Nirrip, Nebo, Iva, Hadad, Allah, Mohammed, Jah, or Jehveh or Jehovah.

Gods of the African tribes: Mumbo, Jumbo, Nyiswa, Geyi, Anymbia, Ombwiri, Onyambe, Abambo, Mwetyi, Guishuah, Nyesoa, Morimo, Devil-Man, Rain-Makers, Taaroa, Oro.

The American savages have: The Great Spirit, Quexalcote, Tezcatlipoca, Gitche-Manito, Nee-ba-naw-baigs, Unktahee.

The Greeks and Romans were the most fortunate of all in the number and variety of their gods. They had: Jupiter, Uranus, Kronas, Saturn, Rhea, Zeus, Hera, or Juno, Neptune, Hades or Pluto, Ceres, Hecate, Cybele, Vesta, Mars, Vulcan, Venus, Pallas or Minerva, Apollo, Helios or Sol, Diana, Bacchus, Mercury, Themes, Horæ, Pomona, Vertumnus, Janus, Terminus, Priapus, Pan, Faunus, Picus, Fauna or Fates, Satyrs, Fauns, Komos, Silvanus, Pales, Silenus, Oceanus, Proteus, Nereus, Tritons, Lencothea, Sirens, Nymphs, Echo, Narcissus, Hesperides, The Muses, The Graces, Iris, Æolus, The Wind Gods, Eos, Aurora, Oros, Cupid, Psyche, Hymen, Peitho, Hebe, Ganymede, Esculapius, Hygiea, Meditrina, Telesphoras, Tyche or Fortuna, Nike or Victoria, Pat, Fate, the Fates, Nemesis, Eris, Enyx, Ferne or Farna, Ate, Litæ, Furies, the Harpies, The Gorgons, Nyx, or Not or Night, Hypnos, or Somna or Sleep, Momus, Morpheus, Mars, Genii, Demons, Lares, The Manes, Heros, Prometheus, Hercules, Jason, Theseus, Castor, Pollux, Perseus, Bellerophon, Achilles, Ulysses, Penelope, Orion, The Vices and the bad Deities.

The Jews have their Jehovah, God, with their sacred books, the Talmud and the Bible.

The Mohammedans have their Jehovah, God, and Mohammed, the prophet. Their sacred books are the Old Bible, and the Koran.

The Catholics have their Jehovah, God, Jesus Christ, St. Mary and many other saints, their Bible and New Testament.

The Christians have their Jehovah, God, Jesus Christ, their Bible, which differs from the Bible of the Catholics, their New Testament, with two versions now extant, differing from each other.

The Mormons have their Jehovah, God, Jesus Christ and Joseph Smith, the prophet. Their sacred books are the Bible, New Testament and Book of Mormons. All leaving in their train the records of distress, woe, war and misery.

The Rationalists have neither gods nor bibles, but drink at the fount of everything that is good, true and deserving.

The different believers call each other, infidels, giaours, heathen, and fight and war with each other, because of the difference of their opinions; and when they find a Rationalist, they all join on him, because he does not believe anything not susceptible of proof.

The object of the following poem is to demonstrate the importance of the religion of humanity.

PHANTASMAGORIA OF THE GODS.

—:—

CANTO I.

Lustrous morning threw her golden beams
O'er the land. On the sky of eastern gleams.
Smiles of living day began. Roses sweet,
Peeping through gems of crystal dew to greet
The swelling tide of life, ever there; birds trill'd
The joyful advent; all nature seem'd fill'd
With rapturous pleasure. Bees humming low,
Kiss'd nodding budlets bursting into blow.
The sun rolled back th' hovering shades of night
To the dark throne of Erebus. Delight
Spread her soft wing, while zephyrs danc'd in play.
On floating ribbons, from the bloom of day.

On the distant landscape, outstretching wide,
Hung the bending sky. The grasses in pride
Looken up to see the bleating lambs at play.
Men were busy, and children gay,
Filling the great demands of work and mirth,
The laws eternal of old Mother Earth.

Stoon in the visne, upreaching mountains high,
Which seem'd to kiss the dome of matin sky,
'Neath which flew shifting clouds in neat display,
To catch the kiss of morning's mellow ray.

There stood a stately hill and rocky nook;
Rolled o'er golden sands a sinuous brook,
Whose course was through a rough and rugged fell,
Which stretched to girth an aged mountain swell,
From where the plain, with matted grasses green,
Bedeck'd with flowers on both sides the stream,
Which lead away to a deep morass dense,
Where the lonley stork abides in self defense.

Emerged from a dark and gloomy glen,
A form of uncouth mien and downcast ken,
Holding in his hand a dead spear of grass,
Seem'd saying to himself: "Alas! Alas!!
Life quivering span of existence
To non-existence; spell of resistence
And conflicts of vicissitudes and aches
Of the heart, and remorse that partakes
Of the night of woe. Why is man possess'd

Of thee? Why is life's consummation dress'd
In acute combinations of nerve
Forces of flesh, sinews and bone, to serve
As receptacles of dire tortures through
Impressive agencies, man never knew?"

"Yes! man was here born without his asking,
Or seeking. Pray why should life be tasking
Him with its burdens, realities, and
Sorrows sad, whose inflictions only end
With the last of him? Oh! bothersome life,
Replete with anguish, contention and strife,
Bid man a last, a long and kind adieu,
And wipe from mem'ry all it ever knew.
On! Death! silent messenger of Peace,
Come thou quickly and break the galling lease
Life hath upon man laid, and in the breast
Of thy omnipotence afford him rest."
"T'would ha' been better, far," Cobolus sighed,
"For man, if he had, before his birth, died."

Vivacious Youth came tripping down a hill,
Beheld Remorse, old and haggard, by the kill
Of Grumble, sitting on a barren stone.
    And making grimace faces at the world
Full of grandeur, excellence, beauty; sown
    By the smiles of Life, through all nature twirl'd.
"Man of venerable age, seem'st thou," the youth
Said, "Deep in meditation bound; the truth
Of nature must have long engaged your mind;
Earth's beauties must, within your wisdom, find
An ardent advocate?" Raising his head
And grim-knitting his brow, the old man said:
"I, from the book of experience learn'd
This word is all deception and fraud, turned
Into gain by the designing; and, man
The prey of man becomes; whoever can
Advantage gain, or oppress another,
Lose not the advantage, though brother,
Or e'en the nearer to him, the father,
And oft', too oft', the languishing mother
Feels but the cold rebuke of neglect;
And yon ebon water doth reflect
The dark currents of man's being, inground
In him, by the fat of nature, found

In all things where life pulsates thro' th' veins,
And animation has uncurb'd reins.
Life, throbbing element, is a curse,
And brings in its train the hideous corse
Of disappointed hope, and in its wake
Strews the bleachen bones of all joy to make
This world fulfill its mission, typified
In these dark stygian waters that glide,
Grumbling, at our feet.   I behold them all;
The red sun so admired, gilds but the pall
Of death, and sends down his mawking beguiles
To allure man, by deceptive wiles,
On in the pathway of torturing life.
See you not, young man, that Nature is rife
With woe, intensified by deception,
Brought into *esse* by life's conception,
Where'er you find life, devouring death,
Grim and goar, is, by his stygian breath,
Reaping the unripe harvest.   Each being
On some other life lives.   Without seeing
You cannot lift your eyes, something eating
The flesh of another.   Thus, completing
The one greatest fiat of Omniscience,
Of unlimited (?) mercy, the essence.

Great God! is this by omnific design?
Are these the workings of thy rules divine?
Or, hast Thou lost omnipotent control
And even up by roasting man's poor soul,
As preachers armed in sophistry oft tell,
And with phantasmagoria paint up hell?
If God be silent to unveil this truth
What canst thou say for it, unpracticed youth?"
"As you have ask'd, I cannot well deny,
To give you my conceptions in reply,"
The youth went on, "You have dethron'd fond Hope
And view things thro' th' eyes of a misanthrope;
Life is the soul of all our joys, I ween,
And woe is not as real as it may seem.
Young life takes all of pleasure in its train,
And woe is but a figment of the brain;
From the blooms of life all animation springs—
We feel joy, or woe, the way we look at things.
In all of life's long and varied train
We have but few ills, or physical pain—

The most come from imaginings of the brain.
We choose between the strains of joy and woe,
And as our mind is bent we have it so.
This world is rife with th' joy of pleasing things;
From the garner of her wealth our pleasure springs:
The clouds, the rainfall and the storms impart
Great pleasure to the true and cheerful heart,
While the golden luster of the sun, at noon,
Dispels the clouds, and dissipates their gloom.
The aged hills, the lichened rocks of gray,
The tiny brook that purls along its way,
The bursting buds, the bough, the leaf of green,
Are mirror'd on the cheerful mind, I ween,
To thrill the soul with rapturous thoughts of fire
Which we need but see to love and admire.
Your fluent tongue with Folly's glibs preside
And make the weaker seem the stronger side.
While jewel'd Truth lies wounded at your feet
To brook the shame of an unworthy defeat;
Prostrate and bleeding 'neath your frown it lies,
With form well chained with Falsehood's galling gyves,
Supplicating the hand of crime to give
The boon that prison'd honor might still live:
While blushing Virtue, chaste, with lips demure,
Sues in the grasp of Lust to be secure.
In vain she pleads while in the monster's jaws,
Yet will prevail, eternal are her laws—
No hidden vice can ever feel secure;
Fair virtue has for every wrong a cure.

Over the mien of the old man a change
Crept, like the visage of a sprite whose range
Was among the demons of the deep.
His hair, as wires, stood on end; and sleep
Seemed never to have tam'd his wild eyes;
Riveted on me with the sad surmise,
That one would feel under the rigid eye
Of a subtle beast, drawing its cold, sly
Coils about him! Dim, and still dimmer, grew
Nature's sweet music. Before my eyes flew
The scenes of all my past time: and, I heard,
As a dreadful shock struck my soul, the word
"Cobolus," Ah! Cobolus, the dreadful.
Me thought, as I again look'd, his fretful
Eye was closer on m˙ drawn and he said:

"Wilford, I ghoul not in tombs of the dead,
But, as something real, walk the earth
And leave my impress wherever the birth
Of evil is. Yes, my magic is feared
Of the monsters. I, the worship'd and rever'd
Am, in the dungeons where there are entomb'd
The subtle vis whose bane has gloom'd
It's thousands; but, I hold a more deserved
Mission, for Wilford, which has been reserved
For all ages past. My mission is to
Reveal the true world to mankind and you
The missuigent for the work must be,
I th' alient of darkness am; in me
Besides the power of giving to man
Life, burden'd with the ills that always ran
Its course, and filled the stream of animation
With woe in all its forms of expression.

My aid was once of earth, a maiden fair
Who sold her manes to demons of despair;
And now she rides upon the wind unseen
And sows, with lavish hand, the seeds of woe between;
And yet life has, for the dead ages past
Deem'd a blessing on humanity cast.
      Mere sophists they,
      Who draw man away
From the deep besetting cognate ills,
That always have fill'd and which now fills
The tide of life, with sickness, sorrow, pain
And death, which follow man with their red train
And their ailments, distresses and diseases.

Man is told these inflictions much pleases
Omniscient Mercy. 'Tis I, Cobolus,
   Whose laugh is the grumbling earthquake,
And breath, the all-threat'ning clouds that focus
   On the trembling sky their shivering flake.
I conquer all save Litæ, a Fay, (2)
Who with alluring ways walks th' earth by day
And soothes the sorrows of the aching heart
By soft delusive smiles, until the dark
Veil is drawn and then it is too late;
   Back comes no true accusing tongue.
Death, man's best friend, can but demonstrate
   The victim to his grave was stung."

On yonder mountain height, above the crag
And cliff, where vultures soar, and eagles lag
On watchful wing to catch the sight of prey,
Is my watch, where no human eye can play
Upon its visne, I sit and ken the world.
There you shall go and 'neath the sky unfurl'd,
See with your own eyes and hear with your ears
Life as it was, and as it now appears.

Wilford there stood aghast.　Prevenient
Admonitions made it expedient
For him to break the thrall that bound him spell
To his stead, but could not, Cobolus well
Knew his vis; pointing his long finger
At his gaze, no longer could he linger
At the spot; his stone heart plastic became
To the will of the demi-god; remain,
He longer could not, but follow'd the lead
Of his captor.　On th' bosom of the dead
Calm he seem'd to float and follow the argus-
Eyed monster where he wist, without logos
Of his own.　A slave he was, and thus he
Relates his experience:　"He held me
By his magic power of will.　A million
Thoughts ran my mind.　The sky, a pavilion
Seem'd, would part its vast folds for our exit.
Its deep sides would come and go; and, then it
Would bend, as though to grasp us in its form.
My mind was daz'd; I felt perplex'd, forlorn.
Upreaching mountain, inaccessible
To man, towered with its impassable
Sides of ascent, high frowning above me.
How to reach its bald brow, I could not see.
While in my mind revolving the great feat
Upon me laid by Cobolus, my feet
Seem'd loosen'd from the ground, which did recede
From beneath me.　Brooks, trees, landscapes and glebe
Pass'd away.　The heighth of the vast inane
Deeps above, great, grand and stupendous fane,
To my aerial loll, sank.　Mine ear,
By resonant fugues enchanting near
Was sooth'd to blissful peace.　The outspreading
Cloud-wing, soft and vaporous, seem'd veiling
Beneath me the glowing landscape.　Th' world
Seem'd falling, to my senses.　It was whirl'd

By some force unseen, from its stead, I watched
Its gentle going: with outspread hand catched
At its sinking shadow, but its presence
There was not. My captor's eye a pleasance
Had reflected, and then I realized
The deception. By some strange, unadvised
Means. I was upon the mountain standing,
And, Cobolus, my eyes was unbanding
Of the delusion that lead me captive
To the wizard's height. There, most attractive
The sight was. Spread before me, in the beauty
Of the real, gilded by the duty
Of this sprite of the yawning cave whose tooth
Whet the sharpest point, on man's greatest ruth,
Was the world. All nations before me arose,
In life, in strife, in struggle and repose.
Cobolus spake. On my astonished ear
Fell graphic words that stung my soul to hear:
"Trolls and spectres are my companions, deep
In fathomless caves tenanted. Keep
The hour, we, when the sable frowns of night
On nature spread its vaporous wing, tight
On the world drawn. There, lorn misery dire,
Of kind and character countless inspire
We, and, thrall all the living with our bane.
In cities peopled dense, and in space inane
We hover around with damps of woe. When
The first life struggle began, then began
Sorrow sore, and as old Time rolls on,
Louder and deeper are the groans that throng
Around the heart; and deafer and deafer
Grows the ear of man, now trained to prefer
The wails of anguish to joy, whose refrains
Send trilling back more symphonious strains
Than the Diapason of Orphean
Notes, trained since nature's sweetest song began."
"Look!" he said. I obeyed the behest
And askance cast my eyes, north, south, east, west.
Beheld I a murk thrown over all the
World. Acuter grew my eye. I could see
The inward workings of humanity
And read with anguished heart, man's destiny.

CANTO II.

"List now to what I say! Wilford, the brave:"
Cobolus said kindly: "And I will save
Many wasteful doubts from besetting the mind
With dark forebodings of the world behind.
Anterior to the days of Drastus,
In the bloom of the grand Antalantus,
Peace, joy, good will reigned in the breast supreme
Of all. All were comely; beauty did beam
On ev'ry cheek. The tongue knew not the guile
Of a wilful sting. From all eyes the smile
Of mirth poured forth a constant stream. Health
And vigor bestowed their priceless wealth
Alike. Disease and decrepitude
Were unfelt. The grim, black, bold certitude
Of deception, wrong, bloodshed and chicane
Had not found a lodgment in the brain
Of man. Two daughters, vivacious and fair,
Bless'd the heart of Karmus; most rare
Were their accomplishments. Minerva learn'd
From them the graces that have erst adorn'd
The name of woman. Matin kisses from
The purest sun-born rays, like dew-drops hung
On th' lips of pouting Beauty. Their graces
Stoop'd to linger where the heart enchases
Virtue with the jewels fair of life and love.
Sweet dreams of memory, that fondly move
Upon the brain and backward carry our
Sweetest balm of life before the dark hour
Of wrong begrim'd the earth with its sorrow
By hideous mien, would drive or borrow
All pleasure from the breast. Oh! that sad, sad day,
When Discontent lead first the heart away.

Ate dream'd the dream of discontent;
The lovely earth and true life serene lent
No enchantment to her restive mind. Change,
New born spectre, that is wot to range
In th' human heart uncurb'd, a victim made
Of this fair bloom of earth; and on her laid
The thought, by skill and scheme, to break the vault
That clos'd within the ebon world the fault
Of wrong. Deep from the Plutonian shore
Roll'd the phantasy back, that "never more"

Would tranquil Peace and blooming health unshent
Reign triumphant through th' world where pleasure went
Unchallenged. Daughter of the shade bent low (3)
Her ebon wing and bade fair Ate go
On journey vast with her beyond the list
Where Helios smiles, and the heavy mists
Of night are never raised; where cognate gloom
Unbroken reigns supreme: where Harpies plume
On wings perennial for sightless flight,
And Neros takes with Pluto fond delight.

The long journey sped, Calæno spread
The festal board, rich laden with the bread
Of that outer world; viands of flavor
Rare and delicate sent up a savor
Captivating to the dullest taste. Fill'd
The goblets were with nectar, cool, and thrill'd
The senses of delight with mellow wine,
Smooth enough in flow to please a throat divine.
'Twas a banquet of the gods of outer place
Where wiles luxuriant retained their place:
Excesses gorg'd th' hour, of every name,
And virtue lay submerged by evil fame.
All the gods of gloomy shade were there,
And manes of Pluto's like, grave, fierce and fair,
Assembled through respect, and honor paid
To the world's self-expatriated maid.
From the darkest darkness, the witch Circe
A nectar brought her, of the jujube.
When it refresh the lips, forgotten all
The past is; and then she thought to enthrall
The maid with evil from the murky shade
That all Pandora's ills on man be laid.
A leathern case of serpent skin was brought
From the squirming locks of Medusa, fraught
With evil. Sprites from the inner precincts came
Waged with evil freight and with evil aim.
Each one, a portion in the serpent case
With thoughts of guile and fingers deft, did place,
For Ate's use, when she should back again
To the fair and blissful earth, direct her aim,
Seeds of sorrow, anguish and discontent.
Many things of guile had the Cyclops sent,
Sickness, pain, disease of every kind,
Decrepitude of frame; deformed of mind;

Avarice, scandal, deception and greed;
Strife, lust, ambition, pride, and all the seed
Of woeful war, incontinence and crime,
Black, of hideous form, whose traces line
The footprints of man with its goar grim,
To fill the tranquil earth with stains of sin
And thrall all animation with the bane
Of woe, dishonor, disgrace and shame,
Which brew and breed in that vast outer sphere
Where kindness is unknown, and spasm'd fear
Rages every breast; where discontent
Stalks broad in every place; the malcontent
Of all grades of wanton guilt and shame,
Of every kind and every name.

The black seeds of murder, some brought and gave:
Pestilence and famine, that fill the grave
With unripe fruit, were brought with lavish hand,
Seeds of lying tongues were sent to curse the land.
Inhumanity brought a fearful load,
And for the slave's poor back the cruel goad
Was there; there, too, came the hideous mien
Of Anarchy, with its lorn clan unseen
In social good; and its missuigent
To th' base and lower scale of life was sent.
Scandal's dark mischief had a special place
Assigned it, where the tongue was trained to trace
The steps of virtue with the mien of vice.
And guilt was ever ready with advice.

Gaunt-eyed Want through poverty's wages wept.
Where Luxury flaunted and Pity slept,
And when the serpent skin was filled with woe,
Ate to earth, on wanton wing, would go,
And as she tipp'd her pinions, soft and light,
    Æolus came, on mission grand,
And ere she sped upon her earthward flight,
    He placed within her outstretched hand
A bag of wind, and Circe came;
"And in this bag of wind I name
All the woes in the serpent skin you hold,"
Circe said, in a witch's language bold,
    "Blow the winds of hardened devil,
    Blow the winds of blackened evil,
    Blow the winds at my command,

Blow the winds through all the land;
Cyclopes follow,
Caves and hollow,
Be thy will obeyed.
Serpent's tooth,
Bringing ruth,
Where its bane is laid;
The darkest ban
Must fall on man."
Thus the Circe said:
"Go with the north winds, go with the south winds,
Go to each nation and clan;
Go with the east winds, go with the west winds,
And blow these evils on man."

The mists were shaken, of the ebon world,
And clapp'd the wing of Jupiter, dethron'd
For younger gods, out from his mansion hurl'd
This ancient god, and he his fate bemoan'd;
And now he sought, from Pluto's reign,
To send to earth his wanton will again;
And all the gods, in that domain of shame,
Imparl'd to curse th' earth, by whatever name.
The Gorgons slapp'd their sides with rage,
The Furies sent a fiercer frown,
And Harpies would with claw engage
A fiercer foe than yet was known.
And Ate quivered on a pendant wing,
With timid will, and would that she could fling
Upon the bosom of the murky shade,
The evils, the Fates had upon her laid.
She would have shrunk, and saved the world its woes,
And virtue of her all-besetting foes,
Could she have thought of Litæ, sister fair,
And earth, with all the pleasures resting there.
Those blessings were denied her memory,
Circe dethron'd, by the subtile Jujube,
While Litæ, angel of the Helois wing,
Would for her sister Ate sit and sing,
Redeeming songs, in plaintive strain,
Imploring the world's perennial spring
To win her Ate back again.
Poor Ate! lost in the dolorous world,
To all recollections of Litæ's love;
Lost to the banner of beauty unfurl'd,

By morn's purple rays, from heaven above
And all of the virtues. where harmony lives.
And all of the blessings Fraternity gives.
She knew but to go as the Fates directed,
Where Trolls might scheme in th' dark undetected,
That Gorgons and Furies might blight mankind.
And Harmony, purge from the seat of the mind.

On the wings of the wind she balanc'd her flight,
Full-freighted with ills to the world of light:
Which ever unchent its bosom had been,
With seeds of crime, contention, or sin.

Through the dark and frore lorn of night
Ate bent her wing on earthward flight,
Remembering not the orcine sphere she left.
Nor e'en the Ord, before she was bereft
Of memory sweet: when it a pleasure
Was to marshal, in her mind, the treasure
Of reflective thought; when beauty into
Beauty blended, and all the world but knew
Fraternal love; unknown all contention
Was; had blissful life alone attention.
As she, unthinking, sped upon her way,
Across the cerule dorse, the smile of day,
Threw a golden hue. Not knowing th' import
Of such a phase, did, like a seraph port
Upon a silent wing in wistful pose:
And while, on pinions loll'd, the world arose
Out of the deep, dark ether, into view.
Her eyes as lanterns glow'd, for ah! she knew
It not. From the fair orient it came,
Rushing onward in a radiant flame
Of beauty; variegated and tinted
In all the aerial hues. Glinted
From its face, as the rose from the half ope
Bud; whose blush of purity as th' hope
Of innocence, borne to a world redeem'd
By man's own worth: in its stateliness gleam'd
With its pristine glory forth, enchanting
The purest thoughts: to man's worth granting
The all unshadow'd praise. Upon the verge,
Where Light's golden arrows sent creeling th' targe
Of darkness to the nether cleft: mountains
Bejewel'd with their bright, laughing fountains,

Wrapp'd. tied and intertied with trenning streams
And rivers vast as silver veins, deep seams
In adamant and beryl cut, turning
Embosom'd lakes and volcanoes burning,
Over and over, as the world roll'd on.
Vast oceans dress'd in the deep blue green, the throng
Of change enchanted. Continents green-dress'd,
Emerged from blue Distance; where on express'd
Man, laughing, joyous and contented.
Guile had not yet tainted his mind; tented
Foes, blood-stain'd and savage, with measur'd tread
Had not won the bays of honor by the dead
In their wake lying. His crowning glory
Was the wreath of honor on the hoary
Head, and the gleam of unshent innocence
Rested on the brow of all; the defense
Of Virtue was Virtue's own sweet smile
That pervaded each continent, realm and isle.

There Scythia stands, with her mellow clime and
Fertile plains; her towering mountains, grand
And inspiring, look down upon Indus
Deep, smooth-rolling, and peopl'd Elymais.
Chalybes in sylvan bowers, their ease,
On Rhea's blessings chime, in tone to please
Orphean ear, songs of plaintive sweetness.
Albania, fair and proud with completeness,
Neath the brow of Niphates and Taurus,
Join with a grand and goodly folk, the chorus
Of good will. Chaos has not on wing o' night,
From Hesperian fields th' dolorous blight
Of discord brought. Lycia smiles, and Cnidos
Sends a kiss of welcome to far Chios.
Deos from the blue waves sends a greeting
To the isles of emerald hue. Meeting
The frore north with Afric's torrid clime;
And look'd, Ate, across the rolling brine,
And there a new world and a new people
Arose before her vision; no steeple
Mark'd a fictitious worship; th' calumet
Of Peace, was in each wigwam, on the fret
Of Cythira floating. Children were train'd
To emulate the fathers gone, who fram'd
The rules of life serene, that thoughts unkind
Should never rape a noble mind.

Palanqua, with her courts and colonades,
Her facades rich and charming esplanades,
Her cuts and carvings, with her paintings grand.
Its architecture and the sculptor's hand,
Leave tracings of a folk of culture well,
That others may equal, but not excel.
Mitla, who can doubt you, standing amid
The wiles of western shore?   Vine-bound, and hid
By trees of stately bow and scented thyme
Thy records lay; on which the hand of Time,
For eons past has work'd and laid his wage;
Yet undespoil'd and bright thy open page,
Where passing man may linger yet awhile,
And cast a thought on Time's receding file,
When man was taken for his sterling worth,
Not gag'd by faith in gods of common birth.
And Uxmel, all our grandest thoughts inspire,
Queen of beauty, which vie with blooming Tyre,
Whose lovely grace abash the pride of kings
And enchace with pride th' true and comely things.
There artful tracings, their own story tell,
Where Science lived, now, but savages dwell.

Ate, a captive stood, half in the glim
Of light, upon a soft and floating rim
Of airy cloud of the world's great beauty.
She remembered not the burden'd duty
On her laid by gods of outer range;
She stood aghast and wonder'd at the change
Before her.   The gods opin'd the reason
Of her delay; the dark ban of treason
Against her pronounc'd was; she heeded not
The curse; she stood, because she had forgot
Her mission.   Circe came with great concern
To know the why she stopp'd, only to learn
That the beauteous earth, more potent was
For good than all the guile and Circean laws
Of evil on the maiden, late of earth,
By witch's subtile wiles, or by the birth
Of other curses in wicked brains conceived,
On her imposed.   By this, the gods were grieved:
And on the wings of sweeping flight through ether
Came to 'quire of the cause of Ate's halt.
Mute and tongueless she stood and gave no fault
Of rule that stayed her there.   A steady gaze

She kept, unmindful of all else, on th' phase
Of life, joyous and serene, before her;
And no plaint importunities could stir
This fair missuigent of evil port.
From her place on the soft and shifting sport
Of hanging cloud. Stung with disappointment
And chagrin'd at her delay, the gods met
Around the stolid Ate, in anger'd
Council, and will'd to know why she langor'd
Thus upon the verge of airy cloud flight,
While the object of her conquest in sight
Of all turn'd her beauteous face around,
In graceful smiles and native bliss profound.
When the gods thus assembled were to know
The why, Ate, in moveless silence low,
Bent her eyes in steady longing, and went
She not upon her mission, orcine sent,
But on the list of darkness there standing,
Motionless, speechless; the gods commanding,
She unheeding. Gave council Apollo:
"That recreant some of the gods below
Were, to strict advice, and by magic spell,
For sorrow potent for guile, impel
Her not to go." Such incantations fell
By witch or wizard, he would not tell.
Must broken be by charms of other guise;
"Circe, witch of outer darkness, arise!"
Austere Apollo said, in tones perplex'd.
"By art of witch and charm subtilly plex'd
Of power, by the fiendish dynamo
In spooks and specter shops in caves below,
Wrought for supermundane use: breathe thy skill
Omniscient in the black art, that the will
Of this stubborn and stolid wench be thine!

Haste to the work and lose no precious time."
Circe, obedient to th' command came,
And by exorcist power sought to name
By adjuration th' witches charm, and threw
Her subtile veil, invisible to view
By human eye, around her, receiving
Back enchantment, fell of veil, conceiving
Of herself, her own vis; captivated
Herself, she was, and by witchcraft mated
With Ate, and by her own was possess'd

Of immobility, hereto express'd
Not in herself. Unconscious she, too, stood,
In admiration, wild with eye she could
Not bend from the rich sun-blessed world that held
A perfection which had not been excell'd
In other spheres. The joyous smile of morning
Sat aglow the blooming face, adorning,
Of terene scenes. The cool, reposing vales,
The mountain peaks and silver stream that trails
The outer disk. The ocean's broad expanse,
The shelter'd bays, across whose face a chance
Albatross might flit a downy wing, lay
Before her, on which her vision would stay.
She was for her weakness, incripated
And was perite. Euterpe invited
To flute delightful tenderness, and win
The senses back to them again, and glim
A ray of hope for the success final
Of this emprise and conceptions primal.

She, too, was entranced and her music fell
From her unconscious lips; refus'd to swell,
As wont, the fairy heart with tuneful bliss,
And in silence lay the world before her,
Which, with impulse new would on her confer
A finite eye, to see the beautiful
Of terene things and the life dutiful
Of man. Euterpe failing, with her lyre
Tuneful, the siren conceived to inspire
With her voice of matchless sweetness, a new
Zeal, and wish for the halting sprites that knew
Not their station. She called with tuneful throat
The mischief-making shades, whose thoughts float
On the vacant air and surcharge all things
With their wishes; at whose dark bidding, springs
Danger in a thousand forms to man's good—
At one sudden impulse, as though they could
Enchant the universe with gleeful song,
Attun'd their dulcet throats to loud prolong
Their wildest praise of the rolling spheroid.
So beautifully filling the vast void
Space before them. The pathless wave of night
Had fled the orient, and morning bright,
A golden trill had sent across the sky,
A flit of joy that dissipates the sigh

Of sorrow; and, brings to man that repose
Of conscious virtue, which he only knows
Who feels its balmy smile. The sprites prostrate
Fell, in form worshipful, to demonstrate
Their admiration of the beautiful
World before them; and there in dutiful
Supplication they revered the sacred
Name of earth; and with zeal and pathos, sang
Its befitting praise. Those thrilling notes rang
Out in loud, deep and clarion strains
That with rage convuls'd Pluto's vast domains,
And caus'd the gods of ebon world again
To imparl, and devise a better plan
To take from the peaceful world its beauty
Of expression; and from man his duty
To himself and his fellow. Megara call'd,
And at his great husky voice, appall'd
Stood all the great immortals of ancient
Rank, on Plutonian shore; but transient
Was their stay: on strong wing of lightning's flight
To the verge of darkness where the pale light
Of the golden car sends a reaching smile
To the sullen ebb and receding file
Of darkness, they sped: and Clio whose fame
Wide spread for wisdom was, was asked to name
The why Ate speechless stood, and Circe
Her enchantment lost; and, motionless she,
Too stood enthrall'd by the world; and, the song
Of siren would, the world's praises, prolong.
Clio wise, then proceeded to relate
That of the ills they had forgotten, Hate,
When filling the case of serpent skin with woes
For Ate's bearing to the world that only knows
Th' smiles of Friendship, Benevolence and Truth.
Bring forth the seeds of Hate, and then with ruth
Will Ate strew the world." Alecto sped
To the inner space of Pluto's reign, red
With things infernal, and with his hand
Of furious reach obey'd the command
And on Ate wag'd the black spawn of Hate.
She smil'd at the accession, but 'twas Fate
That held her yet unmoved toward the earth.

"There is an evil yet, that has its birth
In the brain of man," Clio said. Forgot

.   We have, its importance: it will have wrought
More evil and instilled more discontent
In man, for which more fortunes have been spent
And lives sacrificed, than th' mind can conceive.
This revelation was so great to relieve
The press of thought, Neos, a recess moved
To a time when they could, the improved
Device of contention, potent for ill,
That black evil might yet, the wide world, fill.

CANTO III.

Most interesting was that weird and bold
Story of Cobolus. In th' manner told
As in the deep shrouding mystery
That glooms the mind through the dim history
Of mythical lore, as gods, nymphs, fairies
Cyclops, gorgons, fates, fawns, shades and furies
With those of more familiar names; the most
In use are seraphs, angels, spooks. The ghost
Walks the earth at night. Phantoms and the manes
Of men and devils are upturning brains,
And men and women filled with awe and scare,
To beg the question, humbly kneel in prayer
With eyes upturn'd to heaven blue and fair;
Inportune a being who is not there,
Nor ever was, to help in his behalf
In matters he ought to do himself.
I must not from the story, strange and quaint,
Divert attention. Cobolus spent
Ages in researches legendary,
After facts only known to the very
Subtile of those invisibilities,
That charge the earth with their realities,
And make man feel their presence, yet they feel
Them not. On man's dull perceptions steal
An invisible self, whose form they see,
Yet see not; which he hears, yet hears not. He
Knows it is there, by a sense yet unnam'd.
It is through an impressibility fam'd
In all time by all people, whose tongue
Have voic'd the heart. Whose names have been sung
By all the minstrelsy of note, or time.
Poets have sung of them in verse and rhyme,
Historians have chronicled their deeds,

Sculptors have caught their forms, the painter feeds
His imagery fine, on their furtive wing.
Cobolus was among them, and, we sing
Of him, and through our sentient pen we
Tell his story. The gods conven'd, to see
What evil more, Clio had to bring
To bear on Ate, to force her to wing
Away to the floating earth, and man
Despoil of his pleasures true by the ban
Of the new evil awaited, through the
Conception of the missuigents, free
Empower'd to bring from the murky deep,
All the maladvis'd curses, black, to sweep
The earth of its blooming fitness for man.

All the gods of the shady world, which ran
The list of evils and placed on Ate
The wage, were there, to await the
More subtile curse to come, which, promis'd
Clio, would move sad Ate to be the foremost,
To sow upon the world the source of strife.
Woe, sorrow, murder, and the very life,
Soul and spirit of that potential bane,
That should after encumber man. The name
Of the new curse yet promised had not been
Pronounced. "This curse," Clio said, I ken
Will more prolific be to engender
Discords, and distort the sweet and tender
Chords of human love, than any of the
Wrongs, sad, black and mischief-making, that we
Have, the earth threaten'd yet. It is the bane
Of th' darkest strife; its essence will arraign
Father against son, son against father,(4)
Mother against daughter, and daughter
Against mother. Moreover there shall be
Five in one house; two shall be against three,
And three against two. 'Mong neighbors and friends
Strife it will engender, and often ends
Belief with murder. War, its savage mien
Will blacken. Where'er its name, will be seen
Ignorance and its twin degredation,
Always observable in proportion
To the amount the people have, I name,
With trepidation, this one crowning bane
Of earth, the curse of man for all past time.

This harbinger of woe, strife and crime,
I demominate RELIGION.   It forth
Bring, and Ate will sow it on the earth.

In the assembly of gods arose
A tumult, each would his own name propose
For election; and, Pallas was honor'd,
To make choice and then to send onward,
With Ate, the scourging bane, that would blend
All mankind into hatred and would end
All harmony.   To politeness bred,   ,
Was Apollo; then, arising, said:

APOLLO.

"I am the fair-haired son of Latona,
　　Spring of her commingling embrace with Jove.
Who kiss'd a smile from blue-eyed Medona,
　　And left her to bear and fruit his keenest love,
And bring the silver-bow bearer forth,
An honored god, through an ennobled birth.

She parturient and heavy-footed,
　　Forth went to seek a friendly place of earth,
Where a goddess might find all thing suited
　　To the event of giving a god in birth.
Crete, Cos, and the isle of Ægina,
And likewise was sought rocky Rehnea.

Athens paled and the renown'd Eubœa
　　Where ships heavy-laden with sail and oar
Plow'd the deep wave; and, like Mount Phocœa
　　Shudder'd with fear as well many more
Mountains, cities and isles of the sea
To escape the ban of jealous Hera.

Sea-girth Dalos fear'd to greet Apollo
　　And grant him place of birth, in dread of woe,
Lest the black-sea-calves on her bosom wallow
　　And the tenticled polypus breed and grow
Where man should laugh, till pleading Latona
Breath'd an oath to leave it but harmony.

To it, she pledged a god;—a new born king,
　　Whose silver dart should pierce the side of Juno,
The dam of sin-dy'd Typhon, and bring
　　Her to fierce agony on the ground below,

For wedding evil to evil, to lay
And rot beneath the Hyperian ray.

I am the beauteous, the fair-cheek'd youth,
  Why should I recount my wondrous deeds?
Are they not sung by all the gods? In truth
  The seven-stringed cithara and th' reeds
Relate them and Time's unerring finger
Has written them. In Dalos they linger.

Fire of muses stimulating love !
  Child of Latona and pride of the gods,
My praises roll on the winds as they move
  By Cynthus proud mountain, whose templ'd woods
Me first shelter gave, its laurels first bays,
It honors me now with untrammel'd praise.

MERCURY.

I, the time-honor'd son of Maia,
  Spouse of Jove, am. All bow to me in prayer,
Great wealth and gain I brought to Patria
  And fame to its borders, and arts most rare,
I played to the people in times of old,
And school'd them in getting both silver and gold.

With contrite hearts they lisp my honor'd name,
  And humbly seek my grace in all their work.
I am peerless among the gods of fame,
  In soft-footed prowling when all is dark,
I eclipse them all, as is the belief
I am of all, the sliest, grandest thief.

I cater to all, in their wilder of plays,
  And bring from the tortoise the sweetest strains.
My eloquent tongue subdue man through praise
  And capture his soul through the want of brains.
I rule through the passions, and laughter entail,
And thus gain, while other gods fail.

PLUTO.

My reign is the far deep stygian shore,
  Where manes of the dead are sent for care.
The gods of Tartarus, where ever more
  Shades will be found in contrition and prayer,
But never can gain a glimpse of the light,
But always stay in my reign of night.

EROS.

Most noble Pallas, wing'd, I came from above,
    Where the eyes glowing of Helois remain;
I bring in my breast the swift arrows of love,
    The hearts of the fair are my special domain.
Oh! soften thine ear to the notes of my tongue,
While love's blooming glories forever are sung.

I come with a smile and good wish for them all:
    My quiver I bear with shots for my bow,
The heart I ensnare with love's tender thrall,
    Transfixing the soul with a halcyon glow,
And binding forever in wedlock serene
The lovers who love the sweet pleasures between.

The flowers that flourish within loving hearts,
    And fruit in the season of fervor and youth,
I pierce with the flash of my eye like swift darts,
    And pinion the heart with the savor of truth.
Grant to me the reign of a god upon earth,
And Love will maintain the dominion of birth.

NEPTUNE.

From the foam and flow of the ocean's wide spread,
    Where the dash of the waves and billows are heard,
Where grief is submerg'd by the laugh of the dead,
    Attuned by the voices of Nymphians stirr'd,
To the measure of ecstatic joy to conceive
That Neptune should rule both the land and the wave.

I fashion the storm to the dash of the deep,
    I measure the wind with the bowl of my hand;
The Mermaid's sweet song to the Naiads asleep,
    And Faunies that play on the bloom of the land,
Alike will obey my Omnipotent will,
And each like the ocean will glow through my will.

Just give me the sceptre, and I will command
    With the mien of a god whose bearing I own—
The rivers, lakes, oceans, sea and the land,
    Will flourish with beauty before never known:
And man will rise up with acclaims of delight,
And praise you for the crown my head will bedight.

CERES.

If true gentleness and plenty be your want

To win the sceptre for your honor'd hand,
Then gracious Pallas why you longer vaunt
    Your stay'd decision, and your just command
Reserve? I wear the wreath of plenty; born
Of my desires, honey, meat, wine and corn.

I need but speak, or wave my enchanting hand,
    To bring in profusion, forth, and gladden
The soul, and dearth drive from the famish'd land
    When smitten by the frown-sadden
Elf. If life's comforts you would have bestow'd
Upon the earth, then let me, will, them sow'd.

JUPITER.

Why should I before thy shrine, Pallas, kneel
    And beg for that which of right is my own?
Humiliated in pride do I feel
    To come before you, as you have always known,
I am the chief of all the gods of right,
The crown eternal should my head bedight.

Do not Vulcan, Vesta, Clio, Juno,
    Acknowledge me supreme among them all?
Diana, Venus, Neptune, Apollo
    And all the fairies, nymphs, both great and small
List at what I say, and at my command
Bow in submissive grace, on sea and land.

Shy Mercury, e'en my wishes obey.
    Did not my wiles, Prometheus ensnare?
I caus'd Deucelion and fair Pyrrha,
    Again the earth to people; now beware!
I am the god of gods, and this I ween,
You all will feel, ere long, I am supreme."

This bold speech, a tumult caus'd. All reason
From the convention fled, and bold treason
Against Jupiter was charg'd. Indicted,
He stood before the gods until righted
By an oath of allegiance, or occur
There would among the gods, a fearful war.
A dark cloud of anger besat the brow
Of the twelve, save Pallas and Clio; how
The pending evils they could yet avert,
Opine they could not; yet they, an effort
Resolved to make and the clamor surcease,

If it be possible to maintain peace.
"It is not immortals becoming," plead
Clio, "in war's anger'd fury to shed
Blood, when death cannot ensue. I beg, then,
As Pallas wise can see beyond our ken
To have her cast the voice of who shall reign
And let the gods as friends become again."
Apollo follow'd: "We should not engage
Our immortal strength in battle's grim rage.
Ways of Peace more become our august state
Than frowning war; that leaves a bitter fate
And some must quaff the lees. I will approve
The motion. All the gods immortal, move
To the inner circle, who second me."
All went, save Jupiter, who could but see
Disappointment to his fond ambition,
And would not vow a quiet submission
To the regime, yet would not, then rebel.
He saw he had no following, and well
He knew he could but silent stand and hear
His rights ignored, which plainly did appear.

Pallas stepp'd forward, and with mien demure,
With manners stately and with gestures pure
Said: "Compatriots of th' noble work, hear
Me for th' cause we have espous'd and bear
My feeble words in your memories deep;
Mute should be my tongue; my voice should asleep
Remain, if by fallacious arguing
I should gain a drift of mind wandering
From our common mead. What avail soothing
Words, would be, if, by them we were losing
The good we seek? No accents sweet, of voice,
Should lead us from our duty in the choice
Of noble deeds. The best we say is when
Our words comport with the greatest good; then
We are bless'd in heart satisfactions; bless'd
In the fruits and the results of th' one test
Of conscious right. Bless'd by the great and good,
Bless'd by those we serve, and bless'd by the god
Of eternal meed. Gods of sombre shade,
And of glowing Eos! let facts be laid
Before you, that you may see what of use
There be in the great emprise before us,
To prosecute. The gods of old are dead

To the awe of man. It will not be said
Again, that Osirus, on the throne
Of Light, dispensing benedictions from
His peerless realm, has watchful care of man.
Education has driven him hence, and Pan,
The nymphs no longer his lyre enchant,
And Echo will her voice no longer cant.
Parnassus, the fam'd home of th' gods yet stands,
But the gods have flown and the outer lands
Engage them, and we can never more hold
Man's fond devotions, as we did of old.

Our prince of mystic gods supreme,
Grand Jupiter! I love the same,
And would his glory could arise;
Stars once esteem'd his glowing eyes
Fain not to grace his diadem;
And hallow him as they did then;
His reign hath fled that spacious dome
And left not even faith alone.
But his name now lies at the feet
Of man; who learn'd each gods retreat,
   Snatched off the veil and then expos'd
      Each empty throne, each hollow shrine,
      Each hiding place, where gods divine,
   In former times with pride repos'd
      In some sequester'd solitude,
      In safety and in quietude,
      Where always sleeps infinitude.
When we fled the earth, man in wisdom grew;
Then follow'd happiness. Who ever knew
Man to flourish in blind ignorance?
Stupidity admits of no defense,
Among the mortals; but gods more wise
Can rule his brain only when his eyes
To knowledge are clos'd. Our reign now is o'er,
We must find a god. man knew not before,
A god 'neath whose rule man cannot flourish—
Cannot love himself; nor can he nourish
Fond thoughts of humanity. Does not Greece
Grow insolent and proud, as we release
Our hold upon her? Look at the vain men
With heads erect and steps like bucks of Glenn!
The tranquil smile upon the women rest;
The child sucks comfort from the mother breast;

And damsels flip the frill by laughing toe
And care not a whit but for things below.
Great cities, man has built in reaching plains
And wasteful wreck is sinking stately fanes;
They now repeat the old, old story,
That man comes up as gods go down. Glory
To god is oppression to man. We must
Do our duty, and, to ourselves be just,
And skeptic man bring back to god again,
Or strew his bleachen bones in every plain.
In peaceful pursuits man pursues his way,
He fears not Sharon, Ptah, Pluto, or Fay;
There is a cruel god, who'll bring man back.
I will but nominate and you elect;
'Tis Jahveh, of the wasted plain, I name,
Comes from his nostrils smoke; his eyes a flame   (5)
Of fire shoots; rests his feet on burning coals;
His hair is white, a golden girdle folds
About his paps; great horns grow on his hand,
A two-edg'd sword protrudes at his command
From his mouth; he exclaims with ecstacy,
"I am the god and there is none like me!"
Him we now elect, ran from tongue to tongue,
Of all. May his celestial praise be sung.
And Ate flew on hurried wings to earth
And sow'd with swift and lavish hands the birth
Of all wrong; follow'd in her wake a sigh
And brim'd with sorrow, sad, each tearful eye.

This is the religion that I will name
Unbounded faith in Jahveh, and the same
Obeisance to the pope that some fancied
God obtains from man by ignorance led—
Man's first crude thought is god. His next is reason:
His last and best is of man. 'Twas treason,
In the days when the priests ruled with design;
For man to think or speak beyond the line
Prescribed by some ecclesiarch, and held
By force as mandates of some god, excell'd
By nothing save himself unto himself;
Who reserved all men and things for his pelf,
And for thought divine, in man, wrath untold
Upon his unforgiven head in bold
Assumption was plied. Reason, child of thought,
As a silent monitor, came and wrought

Wondrous reforms.   Now it is, man can,
Without th' fear of flame, think and work for man.
Glorious advent !   Oh! reason, Oh! thought,
Receive them man, and use them as you ought.

CANTO IV.

Never shown virtue more comely.   Few
   Were th' sighs of sorrow, few the signs of wrong.
   Beautiful Litæ, strew'd with her hand
Of heavenly wisdom, the seeds of true
   Manhood through the earth.   From her lips she sung
   Of fraternal love.   Glorious and grand
Arose the heart, mellow'd unto the stream
Of universal good.   Life, as a dream
Of golden beatitudes. ran its peaceful
Course, upon the earth, to a more beautiful
Tenure.   The tender kiss of loving grace
And unmistaken confidence, the face
Of Innocence bejewel'd.   Silver age,
And the ruddy lips of youth, ran the page
Of time, together.   The hearts of all were young.
On th' censorious chord of life was hung
The cithara of harmony.   Man claim'd
The devoirs of man.   That epoch was fam'd
For dependence one upon another.
Smil'd in tender love, the rosy mother.
Walk'd obeisant children with uncowering
Eyes.   Kings and priests were not.   No towering
Fanes mark'd the gloom of day.   Bow'd his head
To no superior.   For ages had
The grand, the glorious and beautiful
Been his instructors; and, most dutiful
Was he to them.   No cloud, his life obscur'd.
From all evil entanglements, adjured
He was.   The earth produced her plenty.   Rain
And harvest came and went, and came again,
In due time; and. man in the bloom of health,
And with pure heart, enjoy'd her bounteous wealth.
Litæ, the fulness of the earth saw, and smil'd.
The face of fair heaven, yet undefil'd
By the noxious eye of deception, sent
A refrain of joy back with beauty blent,
From out the sky, a whisper low was heard.
The listing clouds, by zephyr's wing was stirr'd.

Through the rift in argent flame,
In stoles of white, an angel came,
And as she bent on rapid sail
To Litæ from a golden grail,
She gave a seed of matchless worth.
"Sow this!" she said, "upon the earth,
For Truth it is and must prevail,
I brought it in my goldon grail."
Then rising on the wings of light
She vanished from the pale of sight.

This golden age was not to last,
The cruel Fates, by vile decree,
Commissioned Ate with the task
Of breaking its felicity.
Upon the case of serpent skin, the name
Was writ of Jahveh. When she saw the same,
Ate upon her brow fix'd a deep frown:
And thus old Eblis said: "You are arm'd: down
To the hateful earth, you at once proceed
And with unceasing hand, sow you the seed
In the serpent case held, as you sow, proclaim:
'This seed I scatter in the holy name
Of Jahveh.' Sing th' sad and dolorous song
Of Sirat, Tartarus, of Nox and wrong;
Go with the east winds, go with the west winds:
Go wherever the wild winds blow;
Scatter the seeds of dolorous sins,
Scatter the seeds of Jahveh and woe."
Ate linger'd not; on rushing wing, flew
She to the fair earth, and o'er its face drew
The curtain of sadness and wrong.
As she bent her earthward flight,
She roll'd on the dark waves the song
That came from the shadows of night;
That came from the haunt of the ghouls;
The den of the gorgons, home of the owls:
That came from demons doleful:
That came from dungeons woeful.
She sang as she went,
This withering shent:
"I sow in the name of Jahveh,—
I sow on the ocean and strand;
Sow for sad discord and Jahveh;
I sow on the rivers and land.

I go on the north winds, go on the south winds,
　Go to each nation and clan;
I go with the east winds, go with the west winds,
　And blow these evils on man."

As a vulture from her hidden recluse,
　Beyond the gnarls of the clouds, Ate forth came,
And brought on her wing the withering news
　That Jahveh was ruling, and fire and flame

Consume, would, the soul who felt not the faith
　New born in his breast, and, who would not choose
For Truth's prostrate form, the late conceived myth,
　Jahveh, the adopted god of the Jews.

As earthward she came, o'er mountain and field,
　The seeds of religion she threw far and wide;
Where'er they fell like a shaft on a shield
　It humbled the bearer in person and pride.

Sublime in her terror, she came; the earth
　In its orbit rock'd th' rock of desolation.
Loud thunders crash, and heavy claps the birth
　Of lightning brought, and deep consternation

Fill'd the timid mind of man; and his eyes,
　By th' dust of superstition beclouded,
Saw not beyond the calm and cerule skies,
　Whose glowing face Jahveh had shrouded.

Man converted, fell upon man in rage,
　But for what cause, his judgment could not find,
For selfish meed, the monk, with cowl, and page
　Of doubtful writ, play'd on the puerile mind

And mov'd the passion to a frenzied state,
　Where Reason is dethroned and through the guilt
Of that jealous god, which would immolate
　Fair Virtue on the altar Faith had built.

Such were the curses black-wing'd Ate brought:
　Such was the smiling earth, before the fane
Of Jahveh gloom'd her face with teachings wrought
　With superstition, too absurd to name.

A cloud o'ershadowed Rome. Egypt again
Went back to the shades. Her glorious name

Was tarnished and her prestige soon declin'd;
And helpless now in grief, she calls to mind
The lofty state of the Talmaic rule;
When the world of letters went to her to school.

Now is fading Greece; that smiling Greece now no more.
   The same sun lights her mild and mellow skies,
The same waters gird her firm and rocky shore.
   The same mountains their lofty heads arise.

Yet present Greece, is smiling Greece no more;
   Her glory has departed and her pride,
In valiant deeds now guild her name no more:
   She now but lives to own a failing tide.

The sullen tongue may name Demosthenes,
   And cite the forum of his glory won;
Or may recount the deeds of Pericles,
   But cannot boast of such another son.

Th' face of proud Athens, whose learning and skill,
   Have won from the world its fondest esteem;
Felt th' breath of decay encumber her will,
   And her greatness fled away like a dream.

Where is the glory of Greece, and her isles,
   Where Pindar sang and Sappho loved and wrote?
Her learning now, but thro' memory smiles,
   Which students con and stately scholars quote.

Minerva and the Pantheon combine,
   To render Phidias ever after known,
Less only in the sculptor's art divine
   Compare they to the matchless Laocoon.

Thy stylus stands unrival'd Apelles,
   Thy brush gave Alexander form and grace;
While he was moulding nations to his please,
   On canvass, you flattering were his face.

The learned, yet to Euclid, go to school.
   By theorems get the solid of a hole:
Pythagoras found Deity by rule,
   By numbers prov'd the *esse* of the soul.

When a knight of arms seeks prowess in the field,
   And wish his name enroll'd in verse and song;

His glove intrepid at the latest wield,
And shouts Miltiades and Marathon.

There Æschylus took his majestic flights,
And sightless Homer, by his songs sublime,
Made rules to guide the lesser lights,
That flood a willing world with vapid rhyme.

Design of architect and workman's skill,
On Elgin stone and architraves of gold,
The Acropolis claims our wonder still,
And makes us bow to masters eons old.

Greece spoke thro' her grandeur, lived in her men,
Gilded the pride of the world by her fame.
But now she is weak, as strong she was then;
She lives to-day in the shades of her name.

The stern hand of Time has crumbled her walls,
The night of her past has shaded her domes.
The spires of her fanes her glory appalls,
And Greece has disgraced the name that she owns.

No champering steed snuffs the battle afar.
No panoplied youth feels the pride of his race.
The monk in his stole glooms the face of her star,
And Greece bears the shroud of Greece in disgrace.

Then Truth took its wing of returning flight,
And soar'd away to its heavenly wone,
And left man to wrestle with Jahveh and night,
Till Reason again return'd to its zone.

"I've told you what it was," Cobolus said,
"How the gods conspired before the red
Cross, by Augustine, on his standard rais'd;
And, how the guilt of blood his minions prais'd;
How Fausta plead, and, Crispus lost his head,
A blooming son; and how the millions dead
Begrim'd the earth with ghast and bleaching bones,
How saintly prayers, euphonious the groans
Of skeptics made. The rest, th' historic pen
Has made infamous to discerning men,
Who th' Romish rule behold with sighs and tears
And shrink at the thought of the thousand years
Of darkness they drew o'er the orient,
And of the blood the holy (?) fathers spent.

That was a reign of crime unspeakable,
That made the church of Rome despicable.
That was the way the church became supreme
And wrung from man, subdu'd, the last fond dream
Of hope, and thralled him by religion dire
That batten'd on the rack, dungeon and fire;
Invok'd to aid the tyrants in their zeal
To torture man that god might gain the weal.

The fair earth trembl'd, and the golden cheek
Of Helois dark and sombre became. Weak
Was Astrea then. Fear overshadow'd man;
Strife and contention ruled. Clan after clan,
In contention rose. Divisions and disputes
Prevalent became. Imitated brutes,
More man did, than did they their former selves.
Forgotten all were the joyous indwells
Of friendship of former times. Enmities
Arose; and, crime, heighten'd by jealousies,
Deep intensified by the wage of hate,
Ran rife. Wars ensued and the luster late
Of earth faded away and became lost
In the bewilderments of prayers, that cost
Man horrors immeasurable. The bloom
of fraternal love and light, the gloom
Of Hate arose to kill. Man bow'd his head
In deep and contrite prayer, while, in his red
Hand the haggard cross was held, on his tongue
Lingered husky curses. On the air, rung
The sad, doleful anathemas burning
With ire against all the forms of learning
That blest the earth of erst. Skeptics alive
Were chained in scorching flame, that there might thrive
An obeisant faith in the god new born,
Whose dark reign across the glorious morn
Of man cast a sad and withering blight,
And, on the bright day of knowledge, the night
Of ignorance came. From his lofty state
Man sank to ignominy. Then the great
Was reckon'd by the ingenious skill
He devised of torture, first, and then, kill
Outright, a noble fellow. Those were times
When Faith atoned for baleful sin by crimes.
When Priestcraft ruled the world and Justice slept.
When Religion smiled and Virtue wept.

Dreadful was that night; that long night of man,
Whose deep, unfathom'd darkness never can,
While Time its onward course pursue, repay
The terrors it brought forth.   That baleful day,
We shudder to recall: but the deep cast
Of its hidden wrongs, unnumber'd, will last
In unbroken shame for aye.   Th' sun arose
And smiled and set; but unto man the close
Of day drew nigh; all hope had disappear'd,
And the maw of desolation cheered
Him by fitful dreams.   He lived, but to dread,
The life he held.   The deep and heavy tread
Around the smould'ring embers of his day,
Was but the knell of happiness.   The ray
Of hope had flown.   As a whipp'd slave he grouped
Beneath the lash, his life along.   His stoop'd
Eyes arose but to confront a deeper threat
From some surplic'd monk, who deign'd not to whet
His tooth of woe on coarser food than the moans
Of helpless suspects, whose deep, subdued groans
Were answered by a fiercer scourge, deeper
Wound.   Happy was the day when the sleeper
Slept the sleep of death.   Lorn Misery gazed
On Misery in silence.   Famine praised
The barren rock for succor.   There strong men
Stood in helplessness and in suspense.   When
They asked for mercy, there were sent on high
Prayers for their skeptic souls.   Every cry
Echoed a fiercer pain, a deeper sigh.

Such was Religion in its reign supreme.
Then Happiness was a forgotten dream.
With curses were men's bones crushed, and, the wheel,
The rack, thumb-screw and torch for the weal
Of god were used, which were acceptable
Proofs that they were the most delectable
Savors of grace divine.   The curling smoke
Of victims chained in fire, did invoke
The highest smiles of Jahveh, thron'd on high,
Who smiled to see a disbeliever die.

Nay, shrink not!   Such were the effects that fell
On man, at the hands of Ate.   She well,
Her duty did," Cobolus said.   "Man now,
Through the school of hatred has knit his brow

Against his fellow man, all must allow.
The black shroud of Hate, the world encumbers,
From Afrigah's sunny south to the numbers
Of north wind. From the glowing orient
To the dipping verge of eve that has sent
Its last adieu, of day, across the starlit
Brow of Night, arise one continued wail
Of distress; and, we ask why this detail
Of universal woe, if god be just?
Or is he curbed in his omniscient trust?''

"Throughout all this vast world, animation
On animation feeding. Prostration
Of beings and life is universal.
In the deep, unfathom'd sea, the dorsal
Tribes each other eat, and with gourmand greed
Species on species ravenously feed.
On the land where the zephyrs dance on wing
Of golden beam and sweet throat birds low sing
Of joys spent, one charnal world of woe
Arrest our ken. All above, all below,
The visage sad of deep unrest pervades.
The dark frown of disease and death, all grades
Of life assail. When Death becomes too tame
To be an unwelcome guest, then the name
Of God is spoke and th' genius of man
Is invok'd; and through th' frowns of crime, the ban
Of Popery is laid upon him. The
Joy of which is man's deepest misery.
God wrote upon the face of all, His woe,
And made the world one vast field of sorrow.
The sun paints on the blue and bending sky,
In furtive gleams of gold, a trenchant lie.
All nature presents the face of Janus
To our view. Our beating hearts within us
Bewail the gilding outside of the world,
While neath the film deep lies gnarled and twirl'd
A bitter reality; curse on curse
Arise to blight the every thought. Worse
They are the more the world to us, reveal'd
Is. A hideous mawk the world a field
Presents. All is one vast deceptive grave,
Where Joy is interr'd and Hope made a slave.
Each radiant morn brings new curses forth,
And burden the burden'd frame with the worth

Of anguish fed on Anguish newly born.
Then burning fever makes the flush cheek lorn
And lank. Famine, gaunt-eyed and ravenous,
Stays not his withering breath. Helplessness
Sees his face and dies; dies to leave behind
Lessons to man unheeded, of th' unkind
Hand of wealth clutched in the wan throat of Want,
Tight and relentless. Yet, the poor slaves vaunt
Their price of freedom in the face of Pride
And cry aloud, as other fools have cried,
For God and Liberty. Yet comes there back
No answering joy; no comforting pact
For good; but again new hopes illusive
Spring up and breed thoughts anew, seductive
To the mind, to bear their woes and contend
Anew for something worse, on to the end."

———:———

Up through the fading gray, kiss'd by pearly dew,
On wings of matchless grace, in transit flew
To the verge of Ebon. With fingers deft,
Litæ drew the dense veil of Night and cleft
Its shadows from the earth; back flew its folds.
And in the light afar man beholds
His triumph. Cobolus, in the throes of fright,
Renounced his reign and to the glooms of Night
He sped his way. "It is mine," Litæ said:
"To teach man what religion is." She spread
Across th' sky th' thought. "There is a future,
Grand and inspiring to man; much richer
And more prolific than the proffer'd wage
Through indulgences offered for th' outrage
Of a holy crime. It is felt and seen
In the smiles of love, which will grow and gleam
Through all nature and live through all life.
It will dull th' tooth of Hate and conquer Strife.

It will dress the earth with a new garment
And gild anew the hanging firmament,
With jewels bright. Man's mind will grow broader,
His heart more tender, and friendship stronger,
Than of erst. Great is this coming power.
In this reign of man, a tinted flower
Will impart more pleasure than a sear'd leaf,
A truth, more potent will be, than belief.

A smile will be more welcome than a frown.
Man will strive to upbuild, and not tear down.

There will be more pleasure in joy than tears;
Man will no longer tremble in the fears
Of some great sempeternal inflatus
Devised by priests; the worst is the latest
Conception of the kind." Then on she spake:
"Send back those gnomes of ill. I came to break
That spell of error and enable man,
Blind, deaf, weak and lorn, to resume the van
Of progress, and back cast the heresy
That this blooming earth is the heathery
Of inborn sin, depravity and crime.
Earth is, I came to teach, the crowning prime
Of all excellence, of all beauty and
Grandeur. Divest it of the heavy hand
Of Jahveh, Superstition, Ignorance,
The church of Rome and their concomitance;
Then will man assume his own proper place,
And will Love and Concord, with Truth, embrace
The world." She wav'd her hand across the face
Of space, and, Night disappear'd; in its place
Was seen, shadows lost, of disappearing
Gods. As they went, Litæ said: "Nearing
The end on earth, of their dark reign, they are.
In their place, long so dreadful, the star
Of man is coming, and, with that star all
The blessings of intelligence will fall
To him. Peace will take the place of War; Hate
Will succumb to the smiles of love and mate
To the fulfillment of all good. With the
Ten cardinal virtues, man will be free
To bless his fellow man, and live. Then life,
Glorious pulsation, will fill not th' strife
Of other days; but in a blissful gleam
Flow on in one grand perennial stream
Of felicitude. Then will each tongue proclaim
Aloud the joyful song that man again
Has clasped the hand of fellow man and smiled.
He will vow the vow that will not have defil'd
Innocence, or brought th' name of man to shame.
All the glories of this earth and the fame
Of heaven will be his." While thus she spake,
She stretch'd her sylphan hand across the wake

Of the orient. With strokes of sunlit rays
She wrote in golden words: "Arise, thy days
Oh ! man, are here. Place not, in gloomy fanes,
Thy hope, or thy confidence; but side by side
With Love, Truth, Justice, Mercy and the pride
Of self, place Education, Hope, Good-will
For all, with Charity you will fulfill
Your mission, and, never on earth again
Will Jahveh spread his fierce and sable reign.
His is the reign of dark superstition
Not becoming man or his condition."

"A true religion I have come to bring;
One you can live by, die by and sing;
I bring the religion of living in health;
The religion of plenty and of wealth;
Religion that clasps each man by the hand,
And gleans for their meed the wealth of the land.
The religion of man and of his needs
That follows where'er Humanity leads:
It softens the heart and strengthens the mind,
It makes all alike submissive and kind.
It renders to all the glow of th' day.
It brightens the life, and shortens the way
That leads to the good of celestial bliss
And opens a world far brighter than this.
It teaches no guile; it fosters no sting;
It robes the brow with the garlands of spring;
Harmony spread in humanity's way
In a river of love, coursing away
In grandeur to the broad ocean afar,
In sweet communion of Peace ev'rywhere.

This is religion reduced and refin'd
To serve and promote the needs of mankind.
Religion that weigheth not the belief
That kissing the cross is the price of relief,
But exacts of all this *sine qua non*
That life is the measure of what you have done;
And all must respond to the deeds that he greets
And given the meed for the measure he meets.

NOTES ON PHANTASMAGORIA OF THE GODS.

NOTE 1, PAGE, 84 LINE 18.

" "Twould have been much better far, Cobolus sighed.''

The Kobalds were supposed evil spirits that were believed to infest mines and subterranean caverns. They were supposed to possess the power of poisoning the air of mines, and of corrupting minerals. Prayers were offered up in the German churches against them

But now they cease to bother intelligent miners, who have learned that bad air is produced by gases: that carburetted hydrogen gas, with a small proportion of olefiant gas, produces what is known as fire damps, and that a current of fresh air will do more good in driving out these poisonous accumulations than all the prayers ever offered up for relief.

NOTE 2, PAGE 87, LINE 36.

"I conquer all, save Litæ.''

Litæ was a goddess, the sister of cruel Ate and the daughter of Jupiter. She was by nature the opposite of Ate. Ate was cruel, Litæ kind. Ate a mischief maker; Litæ sowed the seeds of peace and concord, wherever she went.

NOTE 3, PAGE 91, LINE 3.

"Daughter of the shade bent low
Her ebon wing and bade fair Ate go.''

Ate was a goddess of infatuation and mischief. It was her purpose to mislead. All the evils were of her delight. She went over the earth sowing their baleful effects wherever she could do so. Following her was prayerful Litæ, trying, through penance, prayers and kindness, to avert the evils of her sister Ate. This allegory is emblematic of man, who never thinks of repenting until the evil is done and then it is too late. Shame is not usually reckoned as flowing from the act, but results from detection. Then the sinner becomes a devout practicer of prayers.

NOTE 4, PAGE 108, LINE 15.

" 'Tis Jahveh of the wasted plane I name.''

The name of the deity of the semitic race called Hebrews, has gone through several changes, since it was introduced to that people by David, after his abode with the Philistines and Phœnicians. He first was called Jeh, but now it is Jehovah, which Rev. J. W. Chadwick, in the bible of to-day, says is incorrect. When the name became too ineffable to be spoken, it was represented by the consonants, J H V H. When, at length it became customary to fill in the vowels, instead of taking the vowels originally understood with J H V H, they took the vowels belonging to Adonai, or Elohim, making the name either Jehovah or Jehovih. The proper orthography of the word is Jahveh, which is pronounced Yah'weh.

NOTE 4, PAGE 101, LINE 32

"Father against son, son against father.''

"And brother shall deliver up brother to death, and the father the child;

and the children shall rise up against their parents, and cause them to be put to death."— Matthew x, verse 21.

Christ speaking of his mission, says:

"Think not that I am come to send peace to the earth; I came not to send peace but a sword; for I am come to set man at variance against his father; and the daughter against her mother; and the daughter-in-law against the mother-in-law And a man's foes shall be of his own household. He that loveth father or mother more than me, is not worthy of me; and he that loveth son or daughter more than me is not worthy of me." - Matt. x., verses 34 to 38.

Christ denied his mother and brothers.

"While yet he talked to the people behold his mother and brethren stood without, desiring to speak to him. Then one said unto him, 'Behold thy mother and thy brethren stand without, desiring to speak to thee,' but he answered and said unto him that told him, 'Who is my mother? and who are my brethren?' And he stretched forth his hand toward his disciples, and said, 'Behold my mother and my brethren.' "—Matt xi., verses 46 to 49.

"The son of man shall send forth his angels, and they shall gather out of his kingdom all things that offend, and them which do iniquity; and shall cast them into a furnace of fire; there shall be wailing and gnashing of teeth." — Matt , xiii., verses 41 and 42.

Christ promises a terrible punishment. but a good way off; he says:

"So shall it be at the end of the world; the angels shall come forth, and sever the wicked from among the just; and shall cast them into the furnace of fire; there shall be wailing and gnashing of teeth."—Matt., xiii., verses 49 and 50.

"And every one that have forsaken houses, or brethren, or sisters, or father, or mother, or wife, or children, or lands, for my name's sake, shall receive an hundred fold, and shall inherit everlasting life."—Matt., xix.. verse 29.

"If any man come to me, and hate not his father, and mother, and wife, and children, and brethren, and sisters; yea, and his own life also, he cannot be my disciple."—Luke, xiv., verse 26.

"For I say unto you, that unto every one which hath shall be given; and from him that hath not, even that he hath shall be taken away from him; but those of mine enemies, which would not that I should reign over them, bring hither and slay them before me."—Luke, xix., verses 26 and 27.

NOTE 5, PAGE 108, LINE 16.

"Comes from his nostril smoke; his eyes a flame."

"There went up smoke out of his nostrils; and fire out of his mouth; devoured coals were kindled by it."—Psalms, xviii., 8.

"Round about him were dark waters and thick clouds of the skies."— Psalms, v., 2.

"His head and hair were white like wool; and his eyes were as a flame of fire." – Rev., I., 14.

"And his feet like unto fine brass, as if they burned in a furnace."— Rev., V., 15.

"He had horns coming out of his hand, and burning coals went forth at his feet."—Heb., III., 4.

"Clothed with a garment down to the feet, and girth about the paps with a golden girdle."—Rev., I., 13.

"Out of his mouth went a sharp two edged sword."—Rev., V., 16.

"I form the light, and create darkness; I make peace, and create evil." —Isaiah, XLV., 7.

"For I am the Lord and there is none else; there is no god beside me." —Isaiah, XLV., 5.

EARLY POEMS.

——:——

BLESS THE FIRST GIRL WHO INVENTED A KISS.

Of all the beautiful
Things neath the skies,
Is the port of a maiden
With half roguish eyes:
With red pouting lips,
Like cherries so fair,
Which say without saying,
"Take one, if you dare."
I took one. Who would not?
So ripe hanging there,
I could not withstand
Such a temptingly dare.
Then I floated away
On the ocean of bliss,
And bless'd the first girl who
Invented a kiss.
And away, and away,
On the ocean of bliss;
And blessed the first girl
Who invented a kiss.

——————— —

TO MARY.

———

Could angels take a maid's address,
And walk in flesh as mortals do,
Yourself would on my mind impress,
An angel was possessed of you.

There rests on thee a queenly grace,
In charms of sweetest beauty worn,
You seem as of the finite race,
Enwrapped in pure angelic form.

Thy visage cast in beauty mild,
My heart with purest thoughts inspire,
Enthrall me as a trusting child,
And thrills my breast with latent fire.

I cannot change my thoughts with coy,
I cannot move this heart of mine;
With fond devotions of a boy,
I kneel to worship at thy shrine.

WHATEVER YOU SOW THE HARVEST STILL GIVES.

Mawking the mavis of the early spring,
I heard a maiden of her secrets sing,
In the deep dense woods or o'er the sea,
My heart and fondest thoughts will follow thee.

Though withered thy love as the roses may be,
I will wear it still in fond memory,
And ever it shall in my fructuous brain,
Inspire my heart to love, though love in vain.

Thy love like the wind, listeth a while,
Then changing its course, and simply a smile,
Returning to me, when passing away:
As if winning a heart means simply play.

Your game has been play'd; your victory complete,
Your songs were delusive, smiles were deceit,
Your cheeks wore the tinge of a manly grace,
But your heart belied the looks of your face.

You may turn from me, as a victim cast,
Your smiles will not glow, or victory last,
Whatever you sow the harvest still gives,
Though Hope may be crush'd, Memory still lives.

TO LINDA.

Oh! could I waft my thoughts of fire,
　That now inflame my yearning heart,
And in your heaving breast inspire,
　A true conception of the spark
That burns within my bosom true,
With love intense for you, dear, you.

Words are too meager in their sweep,
　To picture love-throbs as they fly:
But true hearts read their language deep,
　As telegraphed from eye to eye,
When love's electric flashes roll
From face to face, from soul to soul.

No linguist can those throbs portray:
　No language can the measure fill:
No limner paint that ecstacy,
　Or speech describe the stirring thrill
That two warm, loving hearts evolve,
When kisses neath four lips dissolve.

THE RIVER OF LOVE.

I walked neath the boughs of a willow,
  Where the currents of two rivers meet;
I stood in the depths of its shadow,
  That fell like a veil at my feet;
I saw the two rivers flow onward,
  In union toward the deep sea;
I watched their two currents flow downward,
  And mingle in felicity.

I thought, as I stood by that river,
  Made whole by the union of two,
Of the rivers that flow on together;
  Of hearts that are faithful and true.
I thought of the deep-seated pleasure,
  The lasting accord and esteem;
That bless the two hearts without measure,
  When love rules the course of the stream.

I thought of the lives that flow onward,
  As rivers flow on to the sea;
Mid flowers and foliage savored,
  With smiles born of sweet harmony.
I thought of the flow of that river;
  How placid its deep waters move;
Full freighted with smiles for each other,
  On borne to the ocean of love.

WHERE LOVE BEGINS.

Love begins with a twinkle and smile;
  A glow of expression;
    A glinting of bliss;
An ecstatic thrill that twirls awhile,
  With a fond impression
    Words fail to express.
Thus love begins.

And thus love ends.
Love ends with th' chill of a lusterless eye;
  A slight cloud of neglect;
    A far away cast;

A word that would shade the birth of a sigh.
A smile that doth reflect
    The wage of a task—
'Tis thus love ends.

THE PANGS OF FIRST LOVE.

You may sing of the winter, may sing of the spring.
    May sing of the long, long ago,
But I have a sweeter, sweet song than all them.
    A song that I sing where'er I go;
A song that I love, and always must sing.
    It is the sweet song of first love.
        The song of first love.

'Twas Sophia's blue eyes that filled me with bliss.
    The eyes that bewildered my heart;
Her lips were unchent by the touch of a kiss.
    Her voice riv'd my heart like a dart,
And made me a slave. I thought not amiss.
    A slave to the pangs of first love;
        To the pangs of first love.

BLESSED IS THAT ONE.

Bless'd is that one who feels and knows
    That friendship is the jewel'd boon,
That Love, its child, forever glows
    Where friendship is allowed to bloom.

Bless'd are those tender smiles of love.
    Which imitate the rose's tint
Of morning, as she lifts the veil
    From off the dew-kissed rose to glint
Away on zephyr wings above,
    To friendship's founts, that never fail.

The smile of heaven always lends
    A grace that moves a constant heart;
And bliss serene always attends
    The love that fills a lover's part.

A SONG.—FROM THE GERMAN.

When melts the white snow, out in the deep forest.
And violets upraise their bright, tiny heads,
The birds, that have slept the cold winter through,
Awake to life again, melodious chords.

When come the spring roses, the heart should be glad,
For this is the time for the smiles of true love;
For only the roses bloom fresh in the spring,
Like love true of the heart. True love from above.

The spring will soon pass, and the bloom will be gone,
The pleasures of May come but once in the year.
Fly the swallows away, but will come again,
Man has only one spring. One only spring here.

LAHLAH.

Charming as the full orb'd moon,
When her argent smiles, the deep blue
Sky inlays with linings chaste. Bloom,
She was of Purity's name. True
As the wave loan'd light of the sun
As he sinks, when the day is done

To rest, was Lahlah; mild and fair;
Modest and retiring. Her
Young fond heart only beat to share
The innocence she could confer
On others, in the linken chain
Of love, that knew no sting, or pain.

She felt that love could not deceive;
And words meant all the wooer said.
'Twould verge on sin not to believe
The vows that on the heart are laid,
When pledges bear them on the wing
Of speaking eyes, like bursting spring.

But like the rose in bower green,
Which sends its sweetness through the air,
To freight the zephyr's wing unseen,
Was plucked by one of wooings fair;
Then on the deep sad ground was thrown,
To wither and to die alone.

˙A LOVE DREAM.

—:—

The day was dying. The soft mellow sun
  Was sinking to rest in the far-reaching plain;
And Leah, content with what she had done,
  In fending the heart from anguish and pain,
Repaired to her thoral 'mid ivy and rose
To find a requital in balmy repose.

The monarch of day soon sank out of sight—
  The limner of nature with aerial dye
Had tipped with vermilion the curtain of night,
  And drew it across the deep dorse of the sky,
That the stars might look down from their chambers above
And pay to the maiden their homage of love.

All nature was quiet; the twittering birds
  Had folded their wings for a season of rest;
The husbandman, weary, returned with his herds—
  The bees to their hives; the swine to their nest:—
Not a ripple or voice from the distance was heard:
No sound broke the stillness; no animal stirr'd.

Morpheus folded his wings o'er the maid
  And whispered: "Good night! Take a short, balmy sleep.˙'
Sweet flowers ambrosial, around her, he laid
  While zephyrs of even on her rosy cheek,
In a sly furtive way imprinted a kiss
And left her to doze in the Eden of bliss.

While Innocence sweet, was thus sleeping alone,
  Secure in the armor of Purity's name,
Watched fondly by stars, in her own sylvan wone,
  Albotine, impassioned by love's cruel flame,
Obtruded himself on her hours of sleep,
And in a soft whisper presumed thus to speak:

"Pray do not reject my petitions of love,
  Nor chide the devotion that flows from my soul:
My heart must adore thee. The bright stars above
  Bear witness of me, that I cannot control,
The feelings that throb in my bosom for you,
They throb for you only, for you, only you."

Now Leah, half waking, bethought it a dream,
  A kind of love waftings, she'd heard not before:
Their thrills were delightful, but false did they seem.

But wished she their musings would be evermore.
The trills of her nerves, the feast of her heart,
That these new-born seemings would never depart.

She wist of those pathose that creep through her veins.
And caused her heart centers to flutter and throb;
Which gave to her senses that grandeur of range,
In feelings exquisite she never had had;
And caused those warm flashes to over her move,
Was the spirit of that which is known as love.

I have loved, she said, and felt the warm glow
That endeared to me mother, a sister and friend,
But from those endearments I never could know,
Or feel the sensations that through my nerves send
That holier thrill; that nameless sensation,
That something that speaks through ev'ry pulsation.

It's the nectar of heaven, the wine of the soul,
It lives in the heart, and speaks through the eye,
It blooms on the lips; it's beyond our control;
Its fountain is purer and deeper, much lies,
Than the fathomless ocean, or blue of the sky.
Deeper than language, thoughts, or even a sigh.

Love has a language, an address of its own,
It's familiar to all, in every clime:
No one can speak it, yet in every tongue
Heart talks with heart, in true eloquence sublime.
It never was learned, and never forgot,
It speaks the strongest when the lips move not.

It paints up the world like the limner of heaven,
It sees winning features in all things around,
It multiplies beauties—all faults are forgiven,
It hears naught but music in each wasted sound:
It softens the heart and nourishes th' mind,
And makes the obdurate, both manly and kind.

Were I the recipient of what I have dreamed,
Or could I but hear that sweet wooing again,
And feel that enrapture, tho' not what it seemed,
That e'er springs up from that idle refrain,
That lies in the chambers of each woman's heart,
I'd be happy in thinking 'twas Love's counterpart.

Its promptings are richer. It brings, I am told,
To the heart that knows not incontinence coy,

A pleasure much greater than treasures of gold,
  More sunlight of life, more streamlets of joy,
More peace and contentment, more food for the heart,
Than the store-house of earth could ever impart.

It plays with the heart of the king on the throne,
  And gleams from the eyes of the queen in the palace,
The millionaire knows it, the peasant will own
  It seems, in his bosom, more like, he will tell us,
The smothered sunbeams neath an o'er pending cloud,
That wreaths to dissever the folds of its shroud.

It's stronger and firmer than fillets of steel,
  Than casements of iron or rivets of brass:
No fetters can bind it, no power conceal
  The stream of its joy as it rushes to pass
To recipient hearts, whose electric fire
Raises humanity higher and higher.

But why should I dwell upon passions like these,
  And dream of the ecstacies Love only knows?
I've rejected the wine, and taken the lees,
  My troth I have bound to celibate's vows:
And promised myself to the people at large,
And cannot, to Cupid, my heart make a targe.

ALBOTINE.

Stir not your young mind with the visions of fear,
  No harm will betide thee, or evil obtrude;
Oh! spurn not the wooings of him who stands here,
  With a heart brimming full of love's beatitude,
When in rapport with you, in the onflowing stream,
Where love knits a web in the bosom serene.

The soft, mellow breeze from Motebo's fair brow,
  Will kiss the sweet smiles that play on your face,
Shall mirror your form as Ouwacha we row,
  And ken the clear wavelets that each other chase:
And when we are wearied of pleasures like these,
We'll weave of the roses a palace to please.

I am the chief of the Mezitine band,
  My trail is the wilds of the forests and mead,
The luxuries of life came at my command;
  My name is enshrin'd in the life that I lead:
To honor I owe the impulse of the brave
And glory is wrote on the flash of my glave.

My sceptre is power, my word is supreme,
The sign of my prowess, I glim in the sky,
The wave of my hand rules my fellows unseen,
And victory smiles at the flash of my eye.
My treasury vaults with bright gold are replete,
I lay with a heart full of love at your feet.

LEAH.

Your ravishing words quite bewilder my mind,
And make me a wait on the billows of doubt;
A bark, on the ocean of destiny, mine,
With my haven obscured on th' whether bound route
And my heart as a captive led on by the dreams,
Of the glistening show of portentous extremes.

The glory you paint in your silver-tipped words,
Come wrapped in a gild of uncertain import;
They bear me along in their glow to the verge,
Where pledges are cast in shadows of doubt—
I wist not to reign in a palace a queen,
Unless in that palace Love reigneth supreme.

The heart of a maiden, when true as its own,
Is dead to the glare of mere glitter and show.
No proffers of station, or smiles it would own,
Are equal the boon of th' gush and the flow;
That came from the soul in response to a train
Full-freighted with love from a true hearted swain.

The heart is not won by great glitter and show,
Though money too often will purchase a bride,
But when she is bought, with the treasures that flow,
At her bidding, it only stimulates pride,
Her heart is uncaptured, her loves reigns supreme
In the heart of another. Thus ended the dream.

ALONE.

The low winds chant to-night. my dear.
A requiem of the past;
Like funeral notes, enthrall the ear.
As they ride on the blast.
I sit me here alone;
Chilly and cold and dark without.
The clouds are gathering fast.
What shrouds of gloom that time has wrought
Within our fleeting past !
I sit me down and moan.

When Love's fond dream infused our breast.
And Hope's familiar gaze
Had calmed the hour of midnight rest.
And glow of happy days
Beamed on our tranquil mind,
The future then in sheen display,
Unfurled her crescent folds.
And sable night was turned to day.
As Time displayed his roles
Of pleasure undefined.

How little then we thought of life,
Of that broad, rushing stream,
Which bears us on 'mid cares and strife.
Resistless, it would seem,
To some dark, dreaded fate;
Our lives away, glide on and on,
Like Time, his trackless course,
Forever bears in measured throng,
His own receding course,
And we may need but wait.

TIME.

——:——

Time withereth the forest leaves,
The oak its lofty head reclines,
And falls its trunk, and sinks to earth;
The dahlia buds, blooms and fades,
The oceans surge, their waters go,
The mountains crumble and decay,
Rocks, rivers, lakes stay but a time,

Then by Nature's fiat decay.
All things celestial and terene
Shall pass before the monarch of Time
And bow to his impressive will.

———— ··· ————· ————

[Written in contradiction of a Rev. Bigot, who asserted that there was no
religion in THE BROTHERHOOD.]

And no religion thou hast said,
    In bitterness of mind,
Can come from noble acts and deeds
    Which in fraternity we find;
No religion where friendship lives,
    Where truth is held most dear,
Where love abides with charity;
    Where is it, then, Oh! where?

We seek the widow in her grief,
    And dry the tears up there;
We clothe the orphans in our charge,
    And hunger drive from there;
The anguish of a brother sick,
    We feel, and with him share,
And yet you tell us in cold words,
    Religion is not there.

In all the varied walks of life,
    Our acts we circumscribe;
In social glee, in business strife.
    Excesses are denied.
To fit man for his sphere as such
    Is our great aim and care;
And yet you tell us in your wrath,
    Religion is not there.

Then where, among the scenes of earth
  Is your religion found.
Secluded in some structure made
  To worship God by sound?
Oh, no! my friends, vain, empty words
  Will never catch His ear;
Though you may pray both loud and long
  It is not there, not there.

You compass both the land and sea
  To make one proselyte,*
And when he's made, he's nearer hell
  Than when you gave him light.
You build for God a gorgeous house
  And vend the gospel there;
The rich go in, the poor pass on,
  Religion is not there.

Religion dwells where love abounds,
  Where friendship never dies,
Where neighbor feels a neighbor's pain
  Through pure fraternal ties.
God smiles upon the golden chain
  Which links men near and far
In one great work of mutual aid,
  He's with such everywhere.

Then hail, all hail The Brotherhood,
  Your mission fill—go on,
Press forward in your noble work,
  Though vaunting bigots frown;
Press on! press on and falter not;
  Proclaim it everywhere;
Let every tongue and kindred know
  Religion dwelleth here.

*NOTE. — "For ye compass sea and land to make one proselyte, and when
he is made, ye make him two-fold more the child of hell than yourselves."—
Matthew xxii, 15.

TRUTH.

There liveth a jewel more precious than gold,
  More precious than diamonds from Africa's field.
Which brighter appears as the wearer grows old,
  Protecting the breast as an armor and shield.

When th' shadow of Time as the mantle of night,
  In silence approaches, performing its task,
Then welcomed the future will be with delight,
  The wearer will have no regrets of the past.

It softens the heart and it brightens the eye,
  Enchases the cheeks with sweet Innocence's bloom.
It wards from the breast the sharp sting of a sigh
  And keepeth the mind from the trammels of gloom.

It honors the brow of both manhood and age,
  And shieldeth from evil the footsteps of youth;
Enriches the mind of both statesman and sage,
  'Who foster with care this bright jewel of Truth.

AWAKE ! MY HEART.

Awake ! my heart, within thy tented bower,
And tune thy notes to cheer this lonely hour,
    And drive my cares away;
Too long thou hast already slept, and whiled
Away the sluggish hours, while Fancy smiled
    Unmindful on her way
    Adown the burnished bay,
Which lies afar without the vision bright,
And quite illumes the dusky folds of night,
    To smile on bursting day.

Awake ! my heart, and view the rushing throng,
Which animates the tide of life along,
    And cheers us on our course,
And becks us to a something undefined
Which we know not, nor care to cast behind
    With Time's receding force,
    Or view its prostrate corse;
We rather bend to that chaotic state
Forward, which the senses infatuate
    And leads us to remorse.

Awake! my heart, my thoughts delusive lead,
The past is gone, the now I do not heed,
          But leer to Fancy's wills;
The woe of others should my soul impress,
And heed as wise the voice of distress—
          That woe the bosom fills,
          The heart with sorrow chills;
And leaves a wound, which Anguish will display,
And by its shadows dims the hopes of day—
          The fondest joy kills.

Awake! my heart, and join the tuneful lay:
A cheerful smile will drive the cloud away
          And dissipate its frown;
The dregs of sorrow coil around the soul
And leave a bane which grow beyond control,
          And weigh the spirit down,
          And weave a baleful gown
Whose folds enwrap the mind with subtle coy,
First animates and then with ease destroy
          The gleam of pleasure sown.

Awake! my heart, and grasp the passing scenes,
An earnest life contains no empty dreams,
          But moves full freighted on;
Man's anguish the world professes to feel,
But man well guardeth first his private weal,
          Which aids him in the throng
          Of busy life along,
Which casts him on the shoaled shore,
Which lies unseen just on before
          Where other cares prolong.

Awake! my heart, and view the onward press,
Ambition's goal, the mother of distress
          Is surging in the strife,
And Pride a jealous pennon vaunts,
And heeding not man's needful wants,
          O'er burdens him in life,
          Makes his existence rife
With anxious thoughts of empty powers
Which haunt as ghosts his waning hours,
          Eludes his grasp through life.

DESTINY.

—:—

Man sows in anguish, reaps in tears,
  And walks in sorrow to the tomb;
He feels the weight of pending years,
  And all their ills before they come.

War, pestilence. famine, disease,
  In turn threaten and assail him;
When one recedes, another comes,
  Which makes his life a troubled scene.

Where'er he looks, which way he goes,
  The dreadful mien of woe is there,
Which makes the past, dark as it was,
  A heaven to his present care.

The present is too fleet for him,
  Too short to start or end a task;
He feasts his mind on future hopes,
  Or gnaws the dead bones of the past.

The sunbeam of illusive hope
  With furtive glances tolls him on,
He works, suffers and endures,
  And learns at last the prize is gone.

When life is through, one backward glance
  Would prove his life a total wreck.
He had but trouble while he lived,
  He came from dust, to dust goes dack.

MY WILL.

—:—

This world. I will to all my heirs,
  In common they may use it.
I give it with the conscious hope
  That they won't spend or lose it.

The seas, the oceans and the lakes,
  The brooks and streams that feed them.
Shall yield unto my heirs, their fish,
  If they will go and catch them.

If they will strive with all their might,
  Both in sunshine and in rain,

The earth will yield to them her fruits,
  Her herbs, and her golden grain.

Each one may have a cosy house,
  With parlor and a kitchen,
A pig, a garden, and a cow,
  If they will work and get them.

One thing more I will bestow,
  While in the mood of giving,
I will that all my legatees
  May make an honest living.

And now I make this last bequest,
  A need, I feel most pressing.
As I have nothing more to give,
  I'll leave with them my blessing.

THE PHANTOM.

As gathering darkness hovers 'round,
  And clothes the scene in shades of gloom,
Without an usher or a sound,
  Then glides the Phantom in the room.

His form defined as where he stands,
  His eyes seem cold and cheerless,
He waves his long and bony hands
  Within the waste of stillness.

He moves about in easy grace,
  And rides upon the floating air,
He turns aghast his wistful face
  In circles waves his jetty hair.

He strokes his beard in deep concern,
  And points his fingers to the floor,
And slowly then he moves in turn
  To vanish through the bolted door.

SILENCE.

There is a day coming whose silence I weep—
Will come in grand splendor to find me asleep—
A day filled with bustle, with sorrow and fun,
After my pleasures and my course I have run.
The world will be joyful, sorrowful, sad,
And bend to the future all blissful and glad,
To leave in the distance the *now* with the past,
Too fleet in its transit to tarry or last,
But wheeled to the rear in measures defined,
For the *now* which glides with time quickly behind,
Will leave in its place the same rattle and roar
That always have marked the days of before,
Whose humming of business and hurry will keep,
While I in my chamber in silence will sleep;
And thus will repose while tempests are twirled,
Unmoved by the sorrows or cares of the world.
As others take pleasure, at travails may weep,
I will, in quietude, slumber and sleep;
While others contend and apply their caprice,
I will repose in deep, deep silence and peace.
Though now I am vieing and pressing the race,
But soon I will yield and to others give place,
Who will, in their turn, their turmoils and strife
Pass quickly the days Time allotted to life;
And thus presseth man on, on to the end
Without comprehending why he should contend.
And thus passeth man to that on-pending deep,
Where he, too, in silence and slumber shall sleep.
The storm winds may madden the ocean and wave;
The battle in thunder may silence the brave;
And pain—reeking pain—may rive the sad breast;
All men in their time will pass on to their rest,
And there with the ages who pressed in the throng,
In silence remain as the world passeth on.

TO LENA.

—:—

Dear Lena, come hence from your play,
  Come hence from your pleasures of life,
Give heed, my sweet darling, to what I may say;
Your heart is as pure and spirit as lithe,
    And true as the lone, cooing dove.
  The soft, trilling notes of your song,
  The glow of your mild, azure eyes,
Accord in their innocent wiles to prolong,
Those joys which pleasurable thoughts improvise
    Direct from the fountain of love.

  The world appears true to you now,
  And all, you think, are as they seem;
No troubles have furrowed your young, placid brow.
And crosses appear, as the sprite of a dream,
    As something unreal and false;
  Truth enwrapt you see in all things,
  And verity smiles ever there.
Sincerity comes on credulity's wings,
Impressing the features of truth everywhere;
    Your heart at deception revolts.

  Your laugh is the guerdon of youth,
  Alternate your tears and your smiles;
Sweet innocence clad in the kirtle of truth.
As shown in your pranks, as in your childish wiles,
    True nature appears in your plays.
  You believe your pleasures will last
  As long as your life shall remain,
That sorrow is transient, has fled with the past.
Shall be no more known, except in the name,
    Consigned to the back fleeting days.

  I wist that your musings were true—
  As true as your confiding heart—
That sorrow and trouble have passed their race through,
And left in their traces Sincerity's chart,
    To guide you in Time's pressing strife.
  Troubles have passed! No, darling child;
  They wane to deceive and ensnare you,
As time flits her wing on the passage that while,
The days of your youth and your innocence through
    Will bring you sad lessons of life,

Lessons now you cannot perceive,
Could not divine them if you would;
That faces are false, dear, you would not believe.
That smiles are deceptive, hearts cold, if you could,
Nor would you such life have revealed.
Things, as they are, scarce ever seem not:
The heart often smothers its fires;
Language is used for the concealment of thought,
And not to express the real desires
That lay in the bosom concealed.

Gay pleasures with time pass away,
While troubles redouble their course;
One loses its station as day follows day,
Increases the other in volume and force.
As life wanes along in its strife,
You often will look for the true—
The facts of your childhood and youth—
Contrasting th' changes behind and before you,
Those dark crowning falsehoods once taken for truth
Will chill then, and shadow your life.

Your burden will oft times seem great,
Your path will be rugged and steep,
May wish for relief from your cares and their weight,
And pray for the rest of that long-lasting sleep
Where joys and pleasures are given.
My child, now heed what I say;
This lesson impress on your mind:
Be true to yourself, as day follows day
Cast all the fanatics and bigots behind,
And keep your eye steady on heaven.

AN EPIGRAM.

Why languish in trouble as time flits away?
Prepare for to-morrow, but live for to-day;
To-day is upon us, yesterday has fled,
To-morrow is always just one day ahead;
Whose wayfaring blandishments beckon us on,
And burden the present with bustle and throng.
Drink not from the past, then, the dread dregs of sorrow,
Nor anguish the soul with the shades of the morrow;
But rather act well the great now as it rolls;
'Tis all man possesses or ever controls.

FRIENDSHIP.

——:——

True friendship, like the evergreen,
  When summer bloom has passed,
Will still retain the flush of spring,
  Through autumn's chilly blast.

And when the winter's sky shall lower,
  With clouds obscure the day,
It still retains its vernal power,
  Unconscious of decay.

LOQUILLIN.

——:——

As matin songs from merry birds
  Rose trilling soft and sweet,
Loquillin sought his daily work,
  And left his child asleep.

Intrusted to a stranger's care.
  In pride, Loquillin vaunts
His happy lot; as working hard
  To meet his family wants,

He toiled for days with cheerful heart,
  And took his guerdon home;
But found, when he had entered in,
  That he was all alone.

He sought the thoral of his babe
  And found it was unfilled.
A stream of horror crossed his mind,
  His heart with anguish thrilled.

He flew then to the matted trees,
  To scan their shaded throng.
He called aloud, "Oh! Mena, where?"
  But echo answered—gone.

With heavy heart he turned within.
  His cot seemed like a tomb,
His footsteps echoed through the hall,
  The sun brought shades of gloom.

The walls were nude of household gods,
  That cheered his heart so long.
He sought the picture of his babe,
  To learn that that was gone.

The grass was growing in the path,
    The sward by growth defiled;
He looked in vain to see a track,
    The footprints of his child.

Neglect was frowning all around,
    His cat seemed shy and wild,
The brood that picked crumbs from her hand,
    Had also missed the child.

He looked aghast in wistful hope
    And list the breezes mild
That wont to waft in days of yore,
    The laugh of playful child.

That bore upon its bosom light
    Her gleeful notes that whiled
The tardy stream of time away,
    Made blithesome by his child.

He asked the sward of emerald hue,
    Where oft in gambols wild,
In sportive glee she tripped its face—
    "If it knew of his child."

"I knew her little lithesome form;
    A fairy, by us styled,
For days she has not been with us—
    I know not of your child."

A wistful ken he cast about,
    In truth the osier smiled,
And told him by its drooping plume,
    "In vain look for your child."

With bleeding heart Loquillin moaned,
    With eyeballs glaring wild,
"Come, robber, take all else I have,
    But leave, oh! leave my child."

"The storm-winds rend the mighty oak,
    Make trackless ocean roiled,
But greater moves the parent heart,
    When it has lost a child."

"Oh! Robber," was Loquillin's cry,
    "Why was your heart beguiled?

Why entered thou my happy home
　To rob me of my child?"

*　　*　　*　　*　　*　　*　　*

Time rolled its weary length along,
　The child grew to a maid,
With mind refluent on her home,
　The cot where first she played.

They came to her with all the zest
　That wins a childish ken,
That moves the heart with burning wish
　To see them smile again.

She found them, but not as whilom,
　Her cat and playthings gone;
Cold strangers had possessed her home
　While she was gone so long.

Now, other children claimed her place,
　Her father, where was he?
She saw instead, a strange old man,
　Delighted at their glee.

She lingered at the curtilage,
　With heavy heart and e'e—
She lisped, as tears stole down her cheeks,
　"Where, father, can you be?"

"My father bore a noble mein,
　He owned an humble cot.
I was so young when stole away,
　His name I have forgot."

"The when my father owned the cot
　I cannot rightly tell.
The litchen grew in wild profuse,
　A tree o'erlooked the well."

"My dreams are of those happy days—
　Those days replete with glee
When love beams shot from father's eyes,
　As I sat on his knee."

The children at each other glanced,
　And asked, "Who can this be,
Who calls in such a mournful strain,
　'My father, where is he?'"

"She wears a sad and wasted form,
 Her eyes have lost their glow;
Is she the child of that old man
 Whose locks are like the snow?"

"With hoary mien and vigil keen,
 Is always on the go;
He walks in sleep the forest deep,
 And wanders to and fro."

"My father planted out that tree,
 He brought it in his hand,
And now its long boughs shelter thee,
 While I a stranger stand."

"Where, tell me, can my father be,
 Is he not here? and why?
Oh! let me see him ere I leave,—
 The world seems whizzing by."

"There is a quaint old crazy man,"
 The children, one replied,
"Who walks the forest and the glen,
 And up the mountain side."

"He sighs a deep and solemn moan,
 We've heard the people say;
He never sits, he never lies—
 He walks both night and day."

The sun ascends the archy way
 And noon-time marks the hour,
Emerges then Loquillin old,
 From out his forest bower.

With feeble steps, but will amain,
 And feelings unbeguiled,
Each day, at twelve, he wanders here
 And searches for his child.

The hour, now, is almost here;
 A moment more, and see
The old man struggle in his task
 To reach the fabled tree.

 *　　*　　*　　*　　*　　*　　*

Loquillin and the maiden met,
 Each caught the other's eye;

"My father!" "Oh, my child!" said he,
"I'm ready now now to die."

A snow-white pigeon took them up,
A nimbus round them coiled,
I saw them pass the azure vault,
The father and his child.

RUNA LANIER,—THE FATE OF A WITCH.

In that dim olden time, that we know well enough,
    When thoughts became crimes, if made beyond rules.
And the people would sneeze when the parson took snuff,
    And sin it was made to have secular schools,
When witches and wizards and devils were here;
    And hell just below if a man disbelieves;
    With heaven above for the foolish at shrieves,
There lived in Glendoven, Miss Runa Lanier.

Miss Runa's ambition subverted her heart,
    And placed her mind under satanic control,
From whom she desired to learn the black art,
    For which she agreed to surrender her soul
To the uses of sin, and the devil as well.
    To serve them through life; to obey and believe
    At the juncture of death without hope of reprieve:
She agreed to submit to the scorchings of hell.

On those were the terms that the devil made witches,
    And Runa submitted to all of the rules,
And receiv'd from his honor a wand and switches,
    Like Moses' rod, once believed by the fools,
And when she would wave them and give the command,
    The wish'd thing would come forth, be it evil or good,
    And obey her desire whatever she would;
As long as she held to the magical wand.

One wave of her wand and will of her mind,
    Would people the forest with bright plumag'd birds;
Would fill the clear water with fish of all kind
    And batten the plain with sleek-looking herds;
She would draw from the rivers, the sportive naiads,
    And fairies from out the deep forests of gloom,
    Which she would disport on the breath of a bloom,
And while away time at the glee of her maids.

At times she would loll on the face of the wind,
Or sit on a long pendant bow of a tree,
With clouds hov'ring over as though they were pinn'd,—
Birds vieing with birds in sweet melody;
Bloom'd flowers of sweetness with colors most gay,
To requite her desire of pleasure refin'd
And quiet the fret of her wildering mind,
By pleasing her ken with their vari'd display.

These pleasures in time grew transient and old,
And Runa would wish for a more pleasant change;
She would long for a smile not so formal and cold,
As those that had come through impersonal range—
She wanted to bask in the florage of bliss
With actual arms encumbering her waist;
With words of warm love to the flow of her taste,
In place of the wiles of Inanity's kiss.

As want to her wishes, a youth sauntered by,
In manly demeanor and favored in looks,
In askance he leered, by a glimpse of the eye,
Her form lovely he saw by a sheen winding brook
Which crept over sand and bright pebble-formed bed,
As kissing the feet of soft swards as it passes,
Neat garland in flowers and matting of grasses,
Well hid from the sun with neat bows overhead.

She lisped not a word, but spoke with her eyes,
And bade the fond youth to abide in the shade.
He came; she was glad, and yet feigned a surprise
That he should invade the thoral of a maid.
Excuses he stammered and vowed it by chance,
He came where a being so charming and fair
As she, as reclined on a moss-covered lair,
Where dahlias and daisies smiled Cupid's defense.

I chide not such blunders, she modesty smiled,
As a neat, artful blush appeared on her face,
Sufficient to give her the cast of a child,
Who knows but that modesty nature would grace;
Runa Lanier knew full well how to act
The charming beguiles of a trained maiden's art
Which neither seems cold nor too warm at the start,
Not yielding, yet yielded, to Cupid's attack.

Dispensed with the use of her long magic wand,
No transfigured lips with impassionate kiss,

Or false formed conception could fill the demand,
   She'd yield all the fairies for love's passioned bliss;
She willed not gay phantoms or visits from pan,
   The pleasures of fancy had cloyed her taste,
   Gay birds and sweet flowers seem'd but a bare waste.
Her eye saw no beauty except in a man.

A hint from Temerity caused him to halt,
   Then Wonder asserted a dominant sway;
'Twixt fear and desire his mind seemed to vault,
   In query he stammered, perplexed what to say
Or do, as the alluring smiles of beauty
   Were stirring his blood and dethroning his senses,
   Abandoned had Reason its wonted defenses,
Leaving him poised betwixt pleasure and duty.

RUNA.

"Come, tarry with me in this sylvan retreat
   And list at the mild, plaintive notes of the dove,
And brooklet's soft cadence, whose murmur is sweet.
   And sip at the fount of the pleasures of love;
Learn wisdom from birds which doff here all their cares.
   And revel uncurbed in the streamlet of bliss
   Where pledges of pleasure are sealed with a kiss,
And Love finds a mate and definitive pairs.

List at the mellow entones of birds' cooing,
   Their warbling songs from neat aeries above;
Take lessons from them in the pleasures of wooing.
   Empassion the heart with the measures of love,
Philosophy cant on Inanity's breast;
   Let Reverie float on the face of the breeze,
   As Logic's cold reason thy being will freeze,
Let Love have dominion—though heed its behest."

He could not opine, well, what others might do,
   If fortune should favor, a deep woodland shade,
A bower well thatched and protected from view;
   Invited to linger alone with a maid
And whisper the breathings of love should it suit,
   With ecstacy float on the face of a dream
   And live in her love, should he fancy the same.
He stood in her presence confounded and mute.

RUNA.

"What omens of evil now rush through your mind,
   What iceberg of woe has congealed your heart veins;

Forget for the present, leave troubles behind,
    To the receding past consign their remains,
Let them be immerged in the dark womb of Time;
    Thou live in the present, thus time is allotted,
    The future before is, the past has departed,
Thou give thyself over to pleasures in line."

"The poet may sing of the 'Pleasures of Hope,'
    Allude to the future well storied in bliss,
May license the mind with poetical scope,
    Yet Fancy will leer to a well-rounded kiss,
When lips bound to lips with the greetings of eyes,
    And heart throbs with heart as though melted in one,
    When ecstacy seizes such mazes of fun,
Who'd quit to chase phasmas or time as it flies?

The streamlet of bliss cannot flow, said the youth,
    If the heart be saddened by sorrow and grief,
The casket of love, like the fountain of truth,
    Can only seem pure when infused with belief.
A jewel when tarnished with foreign alloy,
    Lose cast with the classes to which it belongs;
    When hope is begirded by woe-matted thongs,
The heart cannot fly to the regions of joy.

The glow of thy speech clothes love in neat fashion,
    Thy terms in sweet cadence embellish her well,
You make her appear the goddess of fashion,
    Dethroning the judgment, enchanting by spell
The heart and the mind, bewildered together;
    Transported they seem to the mazes of bliss
    To learn as they journey a lesson in this,
That love is one thing and passion another.

At the shrine of continence I bow, said he,
    I bask in her smiles as my favorite dame,
When wrapped in her mantle of purity free,
    I feel not the sad poignant presence of shame,
I bare not my breast to sensual desires,
    No raptures of pleasure, so fleet on its wing,
    Beguiling to fancy, shall leave me the sting,
That virtue came smiling, but weeping retires.

The damsel who yields to her lover her charms,
    Surrenders the right to a true maiden's name,
Ere wedlock enshrines her within its strong arms,

Or feels not the flow of continence's flame,
Will leave her betrothed for Ameret's embrace,
And forfeit her claims to that holy tie,
With conditions propitious she often wil hie
To pleasures illicit, not heeding the trace.

The purer the mind is the stronger the love,
It gladdens the heart with emotions anew,
Persuasive and gentle as the plaintive dove,
Or kisses on flowers by crystaline dew.
The mother bends over her innocent babe,
And dotes on the infantile smiles of her son,
Two hearts in sweet union, in sympathy one,
Two souls dyed in colors which never can fade.

When heart thrills with heart in true sympathy's chord.
The pleasure of one is the wish of the other:
When pain rives the breast of the other at word,
When eyes cannot veil their anguish, or smother
The feelings of grief, which envelop the two
At the woe of the one, or glow at the turn,
As kindness is trilled on the feelings that burn
With enraptured love flames, such only are true.

It curbs the desire, it softens the heart,
At Continent's shrine a true worship is paid,
Though fortune may frown and old friends may depart.
Youth lose its vivacity, beauty may fade,
Yet Love's true emotions will never grow old,
Its flow never ceases, its source never dry,
It blesses the heart and it brightens the eye,
While passion soon wanes, becomes weary and cold.

I will now hie to my fastness again,
In the dense tangled copse-land on mountain, I crave.
From whose hoary brow may ken the brand plain
Or bend on sheen runnels and th' deep, yawning cave.
Or muse at the edge of a cool, placid mere,
Where cluster, like plexus, the bough and the vine.
And smiling beneath is the gay eglantine,
While Mavis enchants with sweet song the dull ear.

I find only love in my own mountain home,
My heart is betrothed to its copse and the ern,
I love their grand beauty, my sweet sylvan wone,
Where deep-shaded grottos and soft, waving fern

Lend charms to the scenes of my Alpine retreat,
  Where osiers o'erdrooping the waters that gleam
  As they glide to the mere in a rippling stream,
The roebuck to welcome, the heron to greet.

SING.

I love my grand old mountain home,
  I love its breath, I love its looks,
The bloom that smiles on it alone
  I love as do I love its brooks.

The rocks that rib its furrowed sides,
  I love them for their noble state,
As well the rill which down it glides,
  The streams neat kirtled at its feet.

The trees that shade its aged brow,
  Which sheltered me when but a youth,
I loved them then as do I now,
  I love its gray and rocky root.

I love its moan in breezes high,
  I love it when the storm winds blow,
I love from it to ken the sky,
  Which kisses meadlands far below.

The oreole I love to hear,
  And see the roebuck on the bound;
I love the blythe and nimble deer,
  I love to hear the larum sound.

The chase delights my heart as well,
  The bugle and the scented pack,
As coursing through the copse and dell,
  As fly the hounds on heated track.

The eagle plants her ærie high,
  To catch the glimpse of morning sun,
Who paints its streamlets on the sky
  In golden shreds so deftly spun.

I love it for itself alone,
  I love its glens, its gorges deep,
I love my grand old mountain home,
  In sweet repose there let me sleep.

RUNA.

"That mountain home you love so well,
That placid mere, that quiet dell,
That kirtling heath upon its sides,
A recluse where King Ougel hides,
The espaliers of wood-boughs made,
The cascades and the esplanade.
The canons deep, the purling rills,
The cool retreats, the rising hills,
The foliage of the scented thyme,
The blooms that grace the eglantine,
The tarn whose water sparkles, gleams,
Those cool, those clear and trenning streams,
Which trenkle, leap, twirl and spout,
The playful haunts of sportive trout,
Where mountain elfs would wont abide,
And angle in their pearly tide,
The Alpine breeze that listeth there,
To health inspire the mountain air,
The lofty peaks, projecting rocks,
The site from which Angora looks,
And shakes his head, in proud disdain,
At lowing herds upon the plain,
Thou amaret of mountain scenes,
Those lofty peaks, those pearly streams,
Enchantment of a place elfin,
Worhiped as thy mountain shrine,
Now trembling 'neath a witches spell,
Bid them a long, a last farewell,
A wistful glance, a last fond look,
Thou augur from the sable rook,
Whose solo on the breezes roll,
Precursing anguish to thy soul—
List thou, the linnet's ringing note,
Those gifts of nature learned by rote,
The carols sweet of other's song,
Whose dulcet notes its strains prolong,
As vaulting echoes faintly ring,
Trilling softly on the wing.
They sound the requiem solemn knell.
Where all thy terene pleasures dwell.
By this wand's enchanted well
I hurl you all to seething hell."
With warding vengeance at his hand,

He plucked, e'er thought the waving wand,
And by a stroke and word, "*ah vis,*"
He said, "Begone, beguiling miss,
'Tis my command to master this."
And e'er her wish had lost its spell,
He sent the witch headlong to hell.

LAURINE.

I.

Beneath the pendant boughs of a
Brave old oak, on whose branches lay
Memories hushed of centuries gone;
Might have been seen of late years long,
As the sun was sending a last
Kiss of departing day, the cast
Of a wizard, or mystic saint,
In the personage of a quaint
Old man, whom the people called craz'd.
In the rear of the old tree rais'd
A tumulus, a man-made mountain (1)
Tomb of the dead, a grand fountain
Of rare knowledge. Beyond the mound,
Not distant far, may yet be found,
Beside a laughing brook, his hut
Of birchen tree. The wild nut,
With now and then a dainty taste
Of herb, or ripe fruit, plucked in haste
As he wandered from his hut down
The wild brook to the fabl'd mound,
Formed his only diet. The stream
That murmured at his feet in sheen
Ripplets and eddying pools gave
Him drink. The debris from the grave
Of some long lost race gave him food
For his mind. Any eve you could
See him crouch'd beneath that old tree
And in his eager hands tight he
Would hold some simple stone, shell, clay,
Oft'times crumbs of dirt, then would say;
Placing them to his head, strange things,
In language queer, but in such strains
Of eloquence that for hours
One could sit and feel the powers
Within him move. The very soul
Which seem'd chain'd under his control,
Though his tales of incidents, scenes,
Freaks of nature and sprightly gleams
Of thought, clothed with poetic taste:
Grand as the speech of nature, chaste
As the clear blue depths of the sky:

Sublime as the ocean when high
Heaven with her aerial wings
Tips its swelling cheeks with the tinge .
Of evening blushes; sweet and soft
As the first faint whispering waft
Of morning light; ardent as th' gleam
Of Hesperus as the mild stream
Of her face sets evening aglow
And swells with her lustrous brow
Night's approach with animation.
He, a lone one, no relation
Bore he to the people thereabout.
They shunned him and said he was out
Of his mind; talked so strange and queer;
Seem'd more like th' spectre of a seer,
Drawn to earth to fathom the store
Of some mystic truths of hidden lore,
Than a man of flesh. Spread his fame
Through all the neighborhood; yet his name
Was unknown, though for many years
He had lived there; the children with jeers
Dubbed him, "Old Archus." By that name
Spread his legends and his fame.

From his long script of leathern make,
A little stone sometimes he'd take,
And place it to his forehead bare,
And with his hand would press it there;
And then, as moved by mountain sprite,
Upon the stone, sometimes would write,
With a tiny reed, well shapen,
As if by scribe with golden pen;
But no one could his letters read,
Or guess the impress of his reed.

"What name you this?" Lorando said,
    Who gave the leathern polk a pull
And on the ground he caus'd to spread
    A thousand trinkets cypher'd full
Of letters, figures, scrolls and dots,
Which Archus said portray'd the thoughts
Of other things breathed on the brain,
    When they were pressed upon his head;
And each could in its proper train,
    Have all its life and secrets read.

"I name them not," Old Archus said,
"They name themselves as they are read."

These relics form the many pages
That form my great book of ages.
My book goes back to long ago,
When all the universe aglow
With mists, atomic, lay in spell
With Life entomb'd and Force as well,
In Matter: which with supine test,
It was infinitude at rest.

These truths are mine.   I read them all;
I sense them in this rock-form'd ball,
Hard as the adamant and smooth
As polish'd marble.   From a groove
In a large gray azoic stone,
As I was traveling alone
Along the Laurentian hills,
I found it.   Trinkling rills
Had garnished it for ages past.
Vast periods have come and cast
Their records upon it and made

It a living witness in the grade
Of events passing; on its face,
And in its bosom, I can trace
The cause of ev'ry living thing.
I see through it the fountain spring
Of life.   I sense, when the warm wave
Of animation, on the grave
Of cold inanimation, smiled,
And sent young Love to the roil'd
Turgidity of the dark, deep
Depths below, where Death wish'd to sleep:
But, on its vapid face Love breathed:
And Life's womb, fructuous, conceived
And brought forth a living monad.
Anterior to that, all life had,
In the atomies, been dead asleep;
But, through aggregation, broke the deep
Spell that bound it; and forth then came
Sweet budding life; that glorious flame
Supreme, that has aggregated
Into humanity, mated

With passing glories dead and gone
To glories brighter yet to come.

LORANDO.

"Pray good Archus tell us how   (2)
You read such vivid incidents through
The medium of a gem, stone, shell.
Or other relic? Pray you tell
Us how this, your trick is done?
You take, I see, a simple stone
And from it read such stories wild
That daze the wise and please the child.
These strange stories which you relate,
Are too abstruse to demonstrate
By science; yet, we are amused
But hope you will not feel confused,
Or let the ire of your mind
Rebuff our efforts, tense, to find
The powers, which behind you lie,
To demonstrate this mystery."

ARCHUS.

"Cold science, child of vanity,
Asks nature in her verity
To stop as she is on the train
Of progress, and, to it explain
Each simple fact transpiring,
Before the vain aspiring
Student, dull, can accept as true
A phenomena within his view
Perform'd; and like the owl at night
See more in darkness than in light
And what he does not comprehend
Or see, he knows can but portend
To evil; and, like the owl wise
He hoots at them as vagaries.
But as you ask, I hope you'll heed   .
'Tis through a sense these things I read.
This bit of granite, here you see,
    Was taken from Lagullas bold,
Which aggravates Algoa bay
    And makes it hazardous I'm told
For mariners to find their way
Along the south of Afrigah.

It tells my brain, a well-train'd nerve
That eons past, it help'd to serve,
Lamura in her mountain caves:
But now she sleeps beneath the waves—
She sleeps like Atalantus fair
While surging waves roll over her
And monsters of the briny deep
Now gambol in the paven street
Where wealth and fashion once held sway
And nimble tripp'd the carpæa.

If you'll allow my musings range.
I'll now relate a story strange;
'Tis of a maid of ages old,
The story quaint and queer is told.

In the fret of a winding stream,
This filigree I found. Laurine,
Its owner was, she used to wear
Its golden threadlets in her hair;
Bedighting well her queenly brow,
Whose glories and whose anguish now
Transfuse themselves upon my brain:
And, I will through their clear refrain.
Give you her life, exact and true;
Though old in time, the tale is true.
I found it while I was in Greece;
Mount Helicon retains the place
Where Laurine sank in grief to rest:
Those golden threads will tell the rest.

Through kindest nature she was evolv'd
    On whose fair cheeks the sweet kiss of
Heaven, as zephyr's touch, resolv'd
    A gentle grace; and, mild from off
Her fresh and queenly face
Glow'd an angelic grace.

Laurine was kind, with mind serene:
    Fair as the kiss of morning dew;
    Pure as the flakes of falling snow:
Chaste as ice from crystal stream;
True as the vows of Cupid's shrine;
And, none but Love could call her mine.

Once in quiet meditation

She sat beneath a branching tree,
Whose leaves by slow agitation
Sent a solemn refrain to the
Heart. High above the tree she heard
A clear and ringing voice; a bird
Could not have trilled more sweetly
Nor cut those notes more cute and neatly.

From an aerial world palace
Seemed to come a white dove, holding
By a silver cord, a chalice
Of beaten gold; while beholding
It, dumb bound, Laurine stood. With her
Soft silver wing she brushed aside
The feathery clouds hanging 'neath
The dome of heaven, leaving a clear
Sky and smiling sun, the light and pride
Of Nature, behind her. A wreath
Of glory encircled her flight—
A beautiful, beautiful sight!
The soul went out in raptured love
To greet her. What then seem'd a dove
On the air before her standing
She saw slowly, neatly blending,
To the form and similitude
Of a fair and beautiful
Woman. Then her solicitude
Knew no bounds; and most dutiful
Laurine arose her visitant
To honor and to welcome. Her eyes
As sapphire shown. Her cheeks were blent

With kisses of rose and lily;
Lips of ruby. From the deep skies
Of ether, serene and chilly,
Materialized her vesture
Came about her, spotless and white,
Inlaid with a golden lustre
All neatly wove by gleaming light.
Her auburn tresses seemed to blaze
With golden fire, from the rays
Of the sun distilled. Calm she stood
Upon a ball of lucid air,
Angelic was her every mood;
Her smiles were sweet and debonair.

Taking from her chalice bright
An orange-shaped fruit, clear, ripe,
And beautiful.—Unspeakable
Was the scene. With a musical
And charming voice, she said: "Now see
This fruit, my own hand, from the tree
Beatific plucked. Sow its seed,
And whoever harvests th' fruit, need
Fear no guile. The meat thereof will
Every sad and aching heart fill
With joy, and reconcile his life
To the meeds of man. Greed and strife,
On the dark wings of Night, will away
To the by-gones fly, and the day
Of man come forth, garlanded and wreathed
With the hopes of his heart received.
Take it and guard it with care,
The ten cardinal virtues are there—
Virtues, in whose even control
They are, with joy will fill the soul."
Laurine took the fruit; from it came
Ten seeds, labeled TEN VIRTUES. Name
After name, as they dropped, she read.
And then again the fair one said:
"Read aloud and let your voice roll
From clime to clime, from pole to pole,
Let every tongue and nation know
Redemption rests with man below.
Voice ye these mandates from above.

1. LOVE.

"The first grand principle is Love,
    It spans the two eternities,
      And in the heart should reign supreme,
It guards from guile the minds which move
    In concord with its verities,
      And makes the mind of man serene.

2. HOPE.

Hope sees a star, beyond the shroud,
    That fills the heart with dark despair,
      And whispers to the doubting mind:
"Cheer up, for soon the heavy cloud
    Will pass away and then the fair
      Sun will smile and cast th' clouds behind."

3. TRUTH.

"Truth, the brightest jewel in
  Crown of all the virtues, shines forth
    In brilliant grandeur as the guide
To all true excellence.   To be
  Without its guiding light and worth
    Is but to sink 'neath Error's tide.

4. JUSTICE.

"Justice, with imperial mien,
  Demands for all their measure true,
    In wage, in weight, in script and word,
In open deeds and thoughts unseen,
  Each one should have his meed and due,
    And each his merited reward.

5. MERCY.

"Mercy in tears with arms out-
  Stretched, kneels begging, at th' citadel
    Of the heart, for admittance.   Bleeds
Many a sorrowing soul,—not
  For bread, but for pity.   Well
    Be it with those who lighten their needs.

6. CHARITY.

"Charity a ministering
  Angel is, whose ears are open
    Ever to the wails of distress;
And whose great work is administering
  To the needy, and the broken
    Heart, soothing with love and kindness.

7. TEMPERANCE.

"Temperance raps at the door of
  Every heart and claims dominion
    There.   But oft she is cajoled with
Vows, and silenced, that he may quaff
  The dregs of drunkenness, th' union
    Of crime, disgrace, disease and death.

8. FORGIVENESS.

"A forgiving spirit stands the
  Fairest of them all.   To forgive
    Is the divinity within

Man at work.　Give it liberty
　Of exercise.　Hate should not live
　In the heart.　'Tis the vilest sin.

9. ASPIRATION.

"Aspiration is that quality
　Of mind that elevates the man
　　Above the brute.　It will inspire
The mind, if guided properly,
　To all those noble deeds that can
　　Raise man higher and higher.

10. SELF-RESPECT.

"Self-respect should ever be seen
　Reflected through all your days.　To
　　Ride life's tempestuous tide with ease,
You should view with scorn th' horrid mien
　Of vice.　Oh, keep this fact in view,
　　That Honor casts no backward lees."

Thus saying the spectre threw
　Around Laurine as from the sun
A cloak of light, then the two
　At once were blended into one
　　And that one was Laurine.
Then from a thousand throats arose
Acclaims that broke the calm repose
Of nature; and great joy ran through
Every heart, for well they knew
　Laurine by nature was a queen.
A thousand voices join'd in song
And bore the pride of Hellis on.

SONG.

Oh! maiden of Hellenic birth,
　Receive the smiles of Athens proud:
Thy glory will enfold the earth,
　And break the thrall of kingly shroud,
Now let us raise a gleeful song;
And roll the joyful news along:
For Hellis has produced Laurine
To rule the heart of man serene.

There is a tear for ev'ry woe,
　A balm for ev'ry human sigh;
A stream that will forever flow,

From heart to heart with sympathy:
Then let us raise a gleeful song,
And roll the joyful news along;
For Hellis has produced Laurine
To rule the heart of man serene.

The last soft note was borne away
Upon the bosom of the air;
And, lost in the sweet melody
Of Nature's rhythmic voice. The day
Was bright; about the face the fair
Blush of Spring, swam in revelry
And rejoiced at the bliss of twittering
Birds; and the bees' busy murmuring.

By a gentle wave of her hand
Laurine bad her friends good day, then
Returning, they, to their homes. She
Finding kindred echos and grand
Refrains of heart, in a glen
Where a purling brook to the sea.
Wending its way from adown the furrow'd
Cheeks of Parnassus, whose bleak head tower'd

Away to that enchantment, where
The gods saw beauty in the awe
Inspiring scenes o' desolation.
Meditating alone; the fair
One, on the inflexible law
Of mind, near the habitation
Once of gods and demi-gods found
In mountains vast and caves 'neath th' ground.

Sat she, with eyes upon the gay
Flowerets about her smiling,
With her heart attun'd to the low
Rippling brooklet at her feet, they
Enriching her mind and whiling
Away that rich and glorious flow
Of mental enchantment that appreciates
Neither what pain nor pleasure demonstrates.

Her mind refluent on those scenes,
When, unrivaled, up and down the
Rock-ribbed heights of those primeval
Steeps, Apollo strom'd. In his dreams
The rapturous twang and symphony

Of the cithera softly fell
Upon his ear; and trilling to his heart
Back tenderly brought Love's sweet counterpart.

And, in those dreams, as he had seen,
  She saw, that triumph, which is just,
    Over evil.   The dragon fell'd
And the "Bow Bearer" calm and serene
  Kiss the brow of virtue, which must
    Ever reign supreme, be indwell'd
In that heart which for pure sympathy swells
For man, when his soul in deep sorrow dwells.

Laurine saw Time pass along—
  Nature into nature blending;
    Beauty into beauty smiling;
All in harmony moving on,
  As a great river, on, wending
    To the ocean deep, and whiling
Its length along, with nothing to oblend
Its way, till its waters to th' ocean tend.

Her mind had taken rapturous wings
  And flown away to the realms of bliss
    And left her in a revery;
A kind of a perfect rest, where springs
  The sweetest thoughts; the richest kiss
    From Nature's fairest rosary.
Laurine was happy ! Happy in the thought
That all mankind with happiness were fraught.

The blue sky, its capacious wings
  Had spread, like silken canvass, from
    Horizon to horizon.   The
Scenes awoke th' chord that ever springs
  In the breast, where vile passions come
    Not to disturd that sympathy
Of nature serene; which, the universe
Through, pervades, and all its vastness traverse.

Found in Laurine's breast, a resting
  Place, calm thoughts and a welcome wish
    To there abide and bask in the
Sunlight of love, everlasting.
  While thus she mused, the distant clash
    Of arms destroyed her revery,

And fast, she saw, across the plain, afar,
Coming, a steed, caparisoned for war.

As a timid fawn from its lair
  Of grass and wild roses startled;
    Laurine to her nimble feet sprang.
To find a gallant cavalier
  Approaching. His blue eyes sparkled
    With manly valor; his voice rang
Out in clarion strains, as he awoke
Her senses to the horrors, wars, invoke.

Be not alarmed, lady. I came
To bring thee no harm. The name
I bear, to me, unsullied down
An ancestrial line came. Renown
And honor bore it company.
The Gratii trace their family
To that small band of noblemen
Who drove Pelasgi from his den
And proudly spread upon the breeze
The standard of the Hellenes.
'Twas there, he stood, my father's sire
And bore his breast a targe to fire
And sword. Hand in hand, in yon plain
Contended with th' Nervi. The slain
Lay thick about his feet, for well
His aim, each stroke a Nervi fell;
And caused his glave the chamade,
And acclaim of the victory.
Nor can I more inspire my pride
Than thinking how my father plied
The steel to vaunting foe. His name
Was traced, by pens of golden flame,
Upon the rolls of honor. Speak
The archives of that valiant Greek:
And how he did his duty well,
In council and in fury fell.
Nor on the sanguine battlefield
Was Marathon forgot. To yield
He deigns not. He fell with spear in hand,
When striking for his native land.
And these are of his words last said:
"My sire honor'd his sire dead;
A son should live with this in view

To honor self and his sire too,
And as I have no more to do,
The rest I leave, my son, to you."

I live as once he lived: I strike
As once he struck, and, with the might
Of this strong arm, I wield a blade
That no cuirass ever made
Can well resist its cleavage. My
Swift glave has rais'd the courage high,
And cleaved the helmet and the head
Of one who dared to take the lead
Against a Greek to battle bred;
Who strikes for home and sires dead.
'Tis fame that gilds my rising star,
And guides my arm in times of war.
'Twas this that brought me here, fair maid,
To save you, as a cruel raid
Of savage foes has struck amain
In yonder broad and spacious plain.
The foe is there, with shield and spear,
Well skill'd in arms and dead to fear.
His allients will soon be here
To bear thee hence, 'mid shouts and cheer.
My steed stands ready, strong and fleet
To bear thee with his rapid feet
        Far out of danger.
        "My valiant sir,
I fear them not, the grims of war
Can nerve no arm to bear afar
This frame of mine," rejoined Laurine.
"To thus refuse, cause me to ween,
You fear me more," young Gratius said,
"Than the heavy martial tread,
Or athlete arm, that bears the shield;
That speeds the dart, or falchion wield,
Of our enemies; and, on th' name
Of Gratius, cast the shades of shame.
A grim, for all the years of yore,
Was never cast on it before.
He who can cleave the cataphrast,
And lead the charge, can never cast
Upon the cheek of innocense,
The shades that mourn its lost defense."
"Your wits, misguided, mistake me;

I doubt not, sir, your gallantry."
Laurine, with modesty replied:
··I would that you should be my guide
Through passes wild and mountains high,
That I the enemy descry;
Then I will on the battlefield
Achieve more good than you can wield
With armor, spear or trusty glave,
However swift your stroke, or brave;
Now, sir, with haste bring on your steed;
You fleet of foot may take the lead,
And I will follow you afar,
Till danger makes it prudent for
You to surcease, and then the rein
I'll guide and to the brawl amain
And battle wreck, will speed my course;
No harm to self betide, or horse.—
Haste on, brave Gratius, in the lead
Across the heath and fenery glebe
And on amid the battle scene
And I will cease the strife, I ween."
"Should Hellicon his hoary head,
Fold on his side," young Gratius said,
"Or change Cithearous furrow'd brow,
I'd be no more surprised than now;
Firm as the rock of yonder height,
Thou seem'st and strong. To gain in flight
Beyond barbarian reach or trail,
That he might not on thee entail
His wanton practices, refuse
You, your consent. I pray thee lose
No time in idle parleying;
The foe, alert, is rallying,
With all his troop and main
With scout through copse wood and the plain
In search of unprotected prey,
Is now deploy'd. The sun, this day,
Will not have kiss'd the deep green sea
A sweet good night, before the ray
Of virgin hope will have been cast
Of thy own persistence; and lost
In some rude barbarian camp,
Where, rhythmic to the savage tramp
Of revengeful giaours, will be thy cry,

Nay! say not no, but let us fly,
Yes, fly with me, within the lines
Of friendly guard and spear; these times
Are not propitious for maiden
Dreams of romance in love, laden
In feats of gallantry in some
Arcadean wild, where the plume
Waves in the breeze a quiet hour
In safety, in some star-lit bower,
Where philomel, with notes attun'd,
Lend enchantment to th' scenes, perfum'd
With ardent love, on whispers low,
Which sets anew, the soul aglow."
"Nay, Gratius, let thy fears be still:
Desist thou to divert my will;
I must go hence, if blood they spill,
     And soothe their savage natures,
Haste! uncaparison thy steed:
Give me the reins and to the lead.
Across the heathery and meed
     I'll bend my way; and, the features
Of this sanguine test will change;
And Hellis give a grander range.

GRATIUS.

"If thou wilt go, I pray Laurine,
My cuirass take, this poniard keen,
And burnish'd blade, must gleam
     Before the eyes of foemen;
And death must perch on ev'ry wave
Of thy hand. An Amazon brave
Must seem to cleave thy trusty glave,
     And fierce must seem the woman:
Thine eyes must pierce, as darts of war;
And arm must wield the lochabar."

"Thy cuirass, blade and Lochabar,
May serve thee well in times of war;
But I possess a weapon far
     Superior to them. See
This fruit, most beautiful and grand,
Was by the soft angelic hand,
Of the mother of love, embalm'd
     With heaven's blessings. She
Gave me, in days of late,

And said that it would conquer Hate."
"I go!" and ere Gratius brave
Could interpose a word to save
The fair one from a tombless grave,
   Among the maim'd and nameless dead,
As he, with trembling fear suppos'd.
Upon his charger fleet, she posed,
As a sylph royal from the clos'd
   Mountain fastness, where the first red
Tongued rays of sweet morning did gleam
In joyous smiles to bless the scene.
There, with suspended breath,
   Brave Gratius, spellbound stood;
   As through the deep dense wood
She sped her way to death
Inevitable, as he opin'd,
And he was left, standing, there behind.

II.

Moving to keep pace with the shade
   Of the old tree, whose long arms
Outspread, with magic grace, had made
   A shelter 'gainst sun and storms
      For man and beast;
Old Archus, with trepidation
   Wild, with wreathing pain on his face
Depicted, in explanation
   Of its bold and visible trace,
      On brain and breast,
Convulsed with emotion, said:
"I shrink to read, as I have read,
From this bright jewel'd filigree,
   Which annihilates time and space,
To give you facts as it gives me
   Of her young life, that here I trace,
Which on my memory here cast,
Scenes quite fifteen centuries past.
Scenes of horror, scenes of blood,
Which cast upon my mind a flood
Of facts in the march of ages
Which have not upon the pages
Of living history gained a place,
'Till now; and, as I read, you trace
With hand unsoil'd and faber true.

The facts as I will give them, you.
"I see the frail and lovely form
    Of Laurine, borne as the wind; fed
Upon the furious breath of storm
    And rage, to the open cube
Of rough barbarians. Rude
In civic life, and in war
Savage and revengeful; nor
Have they thought of sympathy,
Refinement, or gallantry.
The pure, fair and lovely, find
No considerate balm in the mind
Of semi-beasts, like they. On the face
Of each barbarian I trace
A sardonic grimace-like smile,
As they oblique their straggling file,
To receive in trap the impell'd
Maiden, on to worse than death. Fell'd
Were she to earth. 'Twere better far,
Than thus abide the fates of war
    With barbarians. What care they
For the fruit of fraternal love?
    In their stolid breasts, the ray
Of friendship never caused to move
A heart to throes of sympathy
Or love. Love is a mystery
    To them, that guilds the shadowy
Dreams that slyly flit across th' brains
    When sleep has borne the thoughts away
From the tented plain, where conflict reigns.

Upon the war-trained steed, she flies,
    Of Gratius. In th' distance, the spears
Of well-train'd troops, in line, she spies:
    And, dissipating all her fears,
The fruit does, th' gift of spirit hand.
She gives to Selim his command—
And now, the ground beneath his feet
Seems to fly. Like a roebuck, fleet,
He skims the surface; and, away
Bounding goes to the dense array
Of glittering spears in th' distance seen,
By his accustomed eyes, which gleam
Like red balls of fire at the sight
Of vaunting foe, who smiles to kyke

Such willing prey.
Toward the long and upheld spears,
As whilom Gratius with no fears
Of odds in din of battle met,
Nor glave, nor gleam of burganet.
    He speeds away.
With one bold ramp a fearful fosse
    He clears; but, in the feat Laurine,
The golden apple drops. The horse
    Inspired anew, heeds not the rein
That would now turn his course oblique,
And save his rider from the blight
    Of innocence and death;
Which she with horror now beholds,
As troop by line on line unfolds
Each savage aspect to her,
As borne nearer and nearer
    To their grasp, she is. Her breath
Cut short by transit swift, so that
She cannot articulate. What
Next to do she can not opine,
As she is now within the line
        Of foe relentless,
        And she defenseless.
The steed, she tries to turn to th' right
In vain. He rushes to the fight,
Nor winces he at sight of foe,
But at the tallest plumes will go
With open jaws and frightful teeth,
Agleam with rage. Prostrate beneath
His feet many brave giaours are thrown
To feel the crash of flesh and bone,
As jaws and hoofs are well applied
To those who brave his pressing tide.
Laurine, pale and aghast with fear,
Sees pointed at her breast a spear
Of burnished steel, in the strong hand
    Of a stalwart Gaul, well poised.

Before escapes his lips, th' command
    To surcease, the steed has cloy'd,
By stroke of hoof, his tongue in death;
And makes him gasp, alas! for breath.
But in the whirl pure Laurine falls,
And now in vain for aid she calls.

Young Gratius could not be remiss
In gallantry, in time like this,
Comes he impetuously there,
With visor cast and right arm bare.
One hand has clutch'd th' Damascus blade,
The other on his hauberk laid
Above his heart, and, with the air
Of a noble prince says: "I swear
By the virtue of this trusty blade,
Your best shall fall unless the maid,
That yonder lies, now be unbound,
And she restor'd without a wound
Of honor, or of flesh, to me,
And she go hence as she came, free,
Unsullied, unchain'd and unharm'd,
Or, I will cleave, however arm'd
He be, the head from off the trunk
Of the vile leader of this drunk
And crazy mob.   But if none dare
Confront this glave, unsheathed and bare,
I whiff the sturgid air amain,
In your very faces and proclaim,
To your teeth, to doff that plume
And on your forehead write poltroon.
Who would, like a cringing wretch,
Bow tamely to this glave and stretch
Himself away.   You are a prig,
Unworthy to support the gaudy rig
Of gold embroidered frill and lace,
That skirt your trebble plaid cuirass."

BRANTD.

Avaunt, lad! let thy insolence
    Put not longer the decency
Of speech at bay; of no defense
    Will it admit; such but the spray
Is of effervescent
    Superciliousness.   Behold
One who bore the crescent
    Of success across the bold
Heights of the Cenis, before thee.
    He broke the frore barrier
Of Appenine ice and a free
    Passage made for Gaulians th' fair

Fields of bright Italy to breach,
And revel in love and luxury.
He has stood on the topmost reach
Of Weisshan and watch'd th' tracery
Of the sinking sun fade from sight,
And leave trembling on the cerule height
Of heaven the hanging stars,
O'er chasms deep and moiden bars.
He has stood where the clouds, snow-bound,
Have stoop'd to spread their freight around
The frigid brow of Corinthia.
With noting eyes has watch'd the ray,
Sent burning from the sun's hottest
Fissure to the very topmost
Granule of the Alps, where the Drave
Its first twinkling waters engrave
A crevice, slight, in mountain ice,
Has he stood with ease; and, thrice
The meandering Raab has borne him
Adown its precipitous tide,
In a frail boat of bark and limb,
Without a scratch of hair or hide.

Yea, more, he has delved the grave
Of many and brought the brave
Of other lands in ghastly gore,
At his feet. He has stood before
The cataphrast without a wince;
And with ungauntleted hands, a prince
He has, perforce, from off his steed
Taken, and on the field to bleed
Thrown him. Sir, victory is mine;
And, now you vaunting lad, in fine
Tell me that wench's name, then thine,
Ere I upon this blade entwine
Thy flowing locks; thy flesh piecemeal
To the hungry wolverines reveal
As they to their moky haunts repair
With mouths amoe and eyes aglare.
List thee now; for thy impudence,
I grant to thee but the defense
Of a supplicant for mercy.
Kneel sir, and beg your life of me,
Or, I will lay the stifling treth,
Upon thee of the moils of death.

GRATIUS.

And you demand of me the name
  Of that fair one, the bloom of nature,
Whom you restrain with brutish chain
  Around her slender waist entwined?
    Seek thou first the nomenclature
Of the loathsome, murky cells,
  And there infused, perhaps you'll find,
Where the fungus grows and dwells;
The black, insidious bane
That germ'd to life the very name
That sent you squirming into
  The world, a half made-up hybrid;
Accurs'd by gods and nature too;
With nothing to commend your deeds
But sinks where loathsome vermin feeds.

Her name, so gentle pure and true,
Will never be impressed on you.
But they, the worthy, may but please,
To ask the low and whispering breeze
So soft and sweetly wafted from
    The euphonious shore;
Whence the dew-kiss'd roses come,
  And fulsome morning flushes o'er
Its golden banks, in gleams of love
And on the pillow'd clouds above
        Of argent hue;
        Her name most true,
        Is there enchas'd
        With magic taste.
And I must bow and tell it you?
  Sir, I bow to no power
Save that which comes laughing through
  The impulses of virtue.   Nowhere
Found, save in the flow of pure
And noble manhood.   Secure
You are from such obeisance;
And I from such a grave offense
Of giving you that maiden's name,
That you perforce retain for shame.
You a passion have, it seems, for names.
And, mine, among the other, claims
Your curiosity.   I grant
The wish, and, in it I will plant

Upon your obtuse memory,
A lesson deft and cleverly;
The secret I will soon reveal
To you, but in the revealment
I'll leave in vague, no concealment
O' fact, with this burnish'd point of steel
Within my grasp, sir, you shall feel,
Writing on your panting diaphragm;
With dexterous skill the name I bear:
And by it you will know a man
With nerve has sent a tickler there,
As a pricking thorn to tear
Your vitals one by one and strew
Them upon the turf about you.

BRANTD.

Your insolence befrets me not,
No more than the horn'd owl's hoot
Disturbs the silver moon, as she
Rolls into the cerulean sea
Of ether, and sends a greeting
Smile to the night-gather'd meeting
Of laughing stars. I do but sport,
In mind, at your impudent port.
Would a lion in his lair
Umbrage take at a squeaking mouse?
With his majestic paw, slay her,
He might, at once, with a slight toss,
Sent through the air, for amusement,
Her limp carcass. The slow movement
Of th' mollusk, vexes not the gay
Dolphin disporting in the spray
Of the wind-lashing sea.
Nor do you disturb me
By your despiteful play
On words, malign and coarse.
It would be mete to slay
You now, outright, perforce,
This bright and tickling blade,
And throw your carcass in yon glade
To batten hungry wolves upon,
A feat, deserving to be done.
But as the cat disports
At pleasure with her captured mouse,

And ken it ramp about the house
    Accord with feline sports,
Before she makes of him a meal;
    So I, Gandovan Brantd,
Will pass a playful time with you,
And prick your flesh and hauberk through,
    With falchion keen in hand;
    And make your nerves its keen edge feel.

GRATIUS.

Your falchion I will feel, you say?
Sir! that's a game that two can play;
Come on! and ere half through your part,
You'll find I rule the gestic art.

III.

As lightning from the angry cloud,
    Leaps forth in streams of lurid fire,
And sets aglow the sable shroud
    That hangs around the mountain spire
        And shakes the earth with fear below,
So leap'd the blade from La Brantd's sheath
    And flash'd its burnish'd point in air,
As flash'd his savage eye beneath
    Long tufted locks of sun-burned hair,
        To make the first the final blow.

And with a ferene look of pride,
    La Brantd essay'd a deadly stroke;
Which Gratius deftly turn'd aside
    By cant of arm and counter stroke,
        Which set at naught the savage blade;
And, ere La Brantd could then regain
    His poise, Gratius, by well-aim'd thrust,
His whizzing glave, so swift amain,
    Cut through th' three-plied cataphrast
        And in his flesh a wound he made.

Now wild with pain, wounded in pride,
    His fiery eyeballs swell'd with rage,
As trinkling blood drops, down his side,
    Inform'd him not again engage
        Too rashly th' steel that Gratius bore,
As chaf'd the steed, at bugles' blast
    To charge, yet, by force restrain'd,

So La Brantd chaf'd to downward cast
 His eye on Gratius; who, disdain'd
 His cast, his scorn and pride he wore.

With glave and nerve at his command,
 Young Gratius bore a noble port;
How like, he seem'd, a warrior grand,
 And master of the fencing sport;
  A test of which he could not yield,
But bade the giant come again
 And measure strength with Grecian skill—
A flash of blade and thrust amain,
 Betoken now a sanguine mill,
  Where Pride with Honor vies for th' field.

Right cut, parry, left cut, parry,
 Thrust, guard, head cut, parry, face cut;
Clash, clash, thrust, guard, cut and parry,
 Back and forward, right and left, cut
  And thrust, clatter, clash, round and round,
The burnish'd blades as lightning flash'd;
 Man faced man with cut and thrust;
Like demons mad their sabers clash'd,
 Determin'd both, th' battle must
  Go on till one in death be found.

The nerve of arm and force of will
 Push'd La Brantd on in the contest
With young Gratius, whose matchless skill
 Serv'd well to guard him in the test;
  When death stood ready with a kiss,
For the brow of him who should miss
 A parry, or should fail to guard
Against a thrust, or, strike amiss
 His mark. Long seem'd the contest; hard
  Was th' fight; and neither was remiss.

La Brantd in strength a perfect man
 Seem'd, and, at times his power great
Serv'd to send his sword in hand
 To the very mark, swift and straight;
  But wily Gratius parried well;
Each cut and thrust his ready blade
 Received, and, sent harmless to the side;
With skillful thrust return'd, or, made

A telling stroke with seeming pride;
  Which left effect wherever fell.

Backward and forward, charge defense,
  Face to face, skipp'd round and round.
As in a wild gymnastic dance;
  Moving to the clattering sound
    Of clashing swords and din of shield;
'Till on one knee, young Gratius fell;
  It seem'd his head could not escape
The whizzing blade that seem'd to tell
  Its story. A backward stroke the nape
    Of La Brantd caught, and, then the field

Took the full measure of his length;
  And Gratius, like a young tiger,
Proudly his foot on vanquish'd strength
  Sat, and slowly drew his dagger
    From its golden sheath, and, the crest
That plum'd the head of fallen foe,
  Cut in th' full sight of the great stand
    Of witnesses to the contest.

La Brantd received the agile blow,
  On the medulla sent. The arm'd
Giant fell, not wounded by his foe,
  Nor was he seriously harm'd;
    Only stunn'd; and, he soon regained
Himself in thought and bowing said:
  "Sir, by thy valor, thou hast won
The trophy; 'tis my sever'd head;
  Now take it for it is thine own,
    And let the maiden go unchain'd."

"I am a Grecian," Gratius said.
  " 'Twas always said to their renown,
Though they might fight till they were dead:
  They never struck a foe while down.
    Arise ! your sword resume; the crest
May lie as it is lying there;
  With shield to guard and sword, defend
Yourself like I, with caput bare,
  With blade to bide the nervy hand;
    Shall honor on the victor rest.

Now guard you well; my nimble glave
  Will never rest to leave undone

This work now half-finish'd.   The brave
Twang not the balister unstrung;
 Nor, in the side defenseless, thrust
The envious blade.   Face to face,
 Stroke to stroke, glave to glave, and eye
To eye.   Be ready now, the place
 Where best my blade may pierce I
 Assign'd; now, guard well, you must.

The battle with vigor renew'd;
 Fell fury, black with vengeance reign'd.
Like lightning, each wing'd blade pursued
 From thrust to parry, thrust again,
 The cut and parry, cut and guard,
So swift the eye could scarce detect
 The movements of the savage blade,
That rained and rained so swift and back
 To cut and guard so quickly made
 With whizzing stroke, fast, swift and hard.

A stroke across the grasping hand,
 Sent to the ground the shining blade,
That served so well to guard La Brantd;
 But ere another thrust was made,
 Beneath the folding cataphrast,
A javelin from a coward hand,
 Tore its way; and, young Gratius fell
Wounded in the side, and ran,
 In streams the crimson blood, and well
 He knew he soon would breathe his last.

Rife with indignation, La Brantd's
 Eyes flashed with burning flames of fire.
"Shame! yes, shame on the dastard hands
 That sent this coward spear unfair,

 Into the quivering flesh of this
Valiant youth," he said.   Then he
 Bent over the prostrate form, that
In pools of his own pure blood lay
 Weltering there, and kindly asked, "What
 He could do for that amiss."

"That vile act of an assassin,
 Brutal, savage, and cowardly!"
"Bear me, and lay my hand within

The hand of that most womanly
  Of beings, whom you have detain'd
By force of fetters;" Gratius said.
  "And this is all the boon I ask,
Please hasten ere my soul has sped,
  And think it not an irksome task,
    To let me see the maid unchain'd."

From beneath his ringlet hauberk,
  As they bore the pale youth away
To the maiden, all terror-struck
  At those most cruel scenes that day,
    He brought the apple forth, of love,
Which he, rushing to the scene, found
  Where Selim leap'd the yawning fosse,
Half-buried in the spongy ground
  That caused the trip of bounding horse,
    And caught the damsel in the move.

The wounded youth, with eyes aglow,
  But lips already with the kiss
Of Death upon them, with voice low
  And becoming mild, said: "Fair Miss,
    Let not the pangs of sorrow cross
The portals of thy love-lit heart;
  I lie at the door, 'tis ajar;
Beyond the threshold, the counterpart
  Of all my troubles stands afar
    To greet me.   It is not a loss.

The shadows of departing life are
  Made glorious by the sweet thought
That we have not lived in vain.   There
  Are pleasurable joys in the grot,
    That part the two eternities
Of him who tarries at the tomb
  With the fruits of a well-spent past
Upon him.   They lift th' shades of gloom,
  And usher in a smile at the last
    Flickering spark of fond memories.

How beautiful the silver drops
  Fall from the end of Sharon's oar!
The deep, deep stream in splendor looks
  As its broad, smooth bosom, from shore
    To shore is spread out before me.

This is a pretty boat, only one
  Can cross at a time in it. How
Proudly it bears itself along,
  Parting the wavelets with its prow
    Upreaching so beautifully.

The river is not wide, Laurine,
  But deep. 'Tis not a rapid stream:
But resistlessly on. 'Twould seem,
  Forever to the ocean dream
    Of eternity, it flows;
Bearing down the debris of life,
  To their recompense. The shore,
On the other side. 'Tis all rife
  With beauties exquisite. Seems more
    Like the dream the fairy knows

Of the floating isles in th' golden
  Home of Hesperus, where the sky,
As in the times quaint and olden,
  Came down, with love, to steal a sly
    And furtive kiss from th' cheeks aglow
Of the ocean. There the fair fields;
  The flowery meads; and mountains
Grand, where the flush of beauty yields,
  And quaffs from the gushing fountains
    Of refreshing love that we know.

There bides the soul of love, Laurine,
  The parent tree that bore the fruit
You lost at the fosse, when th' extreme
  Ramp was made. I, when in pursuit
    Of your flying form, found it there;
I give it thee; and to my fate
  I yield, that awaits me for the
Finding." Limp fell his hand to wait
  The call of Sharon. "Now, I see
    Faces of friends awaiting there."

Then changed, as by a magic spell,
  Imposed by some fay or sprite,
From the fair imperial dell
  Of Æaen, where th' matchless
    White-wing'd dove, enchants its sunny face
With song. La Brantd's visage of blood,
  Changed to the smiles of fraternal

Love and kindness. His austere mood
 Had vanished, and a paternal
  Care enthron'd itself with the grace

Of Terpsichore upon him.
 "Unlock those rude chains that entwine
The lithe form of the damsel. Sin
 It is to keep her thus. 'Tis mine
  To recompense with kindness those
Deeds that mar the human soul and
 Wound the flesh with inflictions;" said
La Brandt to his uncouth command,
 That stood about already wed,
  Through Laurine's looks to Love's repose.

"Fair one, roll back to the Scythian
 Cave, those frore thoughts of my mind,
That have erstwhile my soul within
 Disturbed; and, let my yearnings find
  A heaven in thy smiles divine;
And may my hope to thee arise
 To blessings; as the daffodil
Bends to the rising sun its eyes,
 So let me cast my hope and dwell
  My fondest heart on thee as mine."

"Oh! let the cimmerian caves,
 Unbolt their savage doors and drink
From thee, those warm refreshing rays
 Of fraternity; and, to th' brink
  Of hate bear the tidings serene
Of love; that all may see and feel
 That fraternal peace brings to the
Mind heaven's most bounteous weal;
 And to the soul that wills it, free
  Range to bask in Love's fond domain."

Thy fair cheeks make me wish that I,
 On sylphan pinions could arise,
And through the stars that jet the sky,
 Look down on thee with million eyes;
  And, with each eye, drink in the whole
Of thy loveliness and bear it,
 Fraught with all thy goodness and worth,
To where the morning light was lit,

And Nature wraught the coming birth
  Of man and breathed on him a soul.

"What ill-formed creature could have moved
  The spring germs of life, to bring
The seeds of hatred to the groved
  Garden of man; and in the spring
  Of his existence make him more
A reveling beast of lust and crime
  Than a man, with the endowments
Of all those qualities sublime,
    That make th' world the embodiment
    Of loveliness on sea and shore?"

"Laurine, erst you go forth to show
  To the world, how it can conquer hate
With love, war with peace, and to sow
  The seeds of kindness in the late
    Soil of greed, woe and corruption:
Tear, first, I pray you, from the priest
  His cowl, and from the monk his stole
And mitre. Crime is hated least
    With them, when it enters on th' role
    O' papal rule and man's subjection.

The tears that trinkle down the cheeks
  Of Distress, and, the moan that breaks
The sorrowing heart, and, that wrecks
  The breast with pain, with them awakes
    No kindred throb of sympathy;
There are no binding ties for him
  Who wears the stole. No wife, no child
He calls his own; no joy within
    Save that of chanting anthems wild
    In chorus at the litany.

Arise, fair maiden! be thou free.
  The partings of thine azure eyes
Have won my heart and conquer'd me.
  My hand shall not again arise
    Against my fellowman in hate.
By thy demeanor kind have done
  More wondrous deeds of prowess, than
Could th' hundred hands of Ægæan.
    My sword and spear shall rest, nor, can
    The sound of bugle stimulate

"My nerves again for war.   Command,
  And I will be thy willing slave.
Poor boy!   Noble Gratius!   The hand
  That caused the blood of this young brave
    Knight of Honor, to flow by stealth
Of spear, should be tabooed with Shame
  For decency should fence her brow
Against the wretch.   Ill be the fame
  Of him who strikes a secret blow,
    When one cannot defend himself.

"Poor Gratius moves not.   He is dead!
  'Tis scarce an hour since this youth
Inspired my strong arm to heed
  His matchless skill: but now, in ruth
    I bend my eyes on him, stark, dead!
The fire has fled his hazel eyes;
  His cheeks have lost their manly pride,
That spake through them; and, now he lies
  Speechless before me!   How he died!
    Pulseless now as the glave he sped."

The looks of love, that bless'd the eyes
  And flush'd the glowing cheeks of bloom,
Had fled Laurine's face; and, their emprise
  Of good, had turn'd to looks of gloom—
    Sorrow, deep, her sweet smile did shade:
She stood in silence and in grief
  Beside the pale and pulseless youth:
Beat her aching heart for relief;
  But her soul was engulf'd in ruth,
    And woe intense did her thoughts invade.

Beneath an oak they delved his grave;
  His visor on his face was drawn;
The honors of a soldier brave,
  By all the warriors there were shown:
    Thus he was laid away to rest.
Laurine a little stone had placed
  To mark the resting of his head;
A wild syringa, sweet and chaste,
  She planted on his grave and said,
    "He died for me; for me oppress'd."

"The trees, Laurine, are golden-tipp'd;
  The sun has sent his kiss adieu;

The bee, the honied bloom has sipp'd,
And from the shades of night withdrew,
And soon the blooming face of earth
Will be enwrapp'd with sable gloom;
And we will have to brook the stream
Of nightfall dark, unless we soon
Depart for th' camp where we can dream
Of floating hours of song and mirth."

"There are no hours of mirth for me;
No song can cheer my heart again;
The grave has won its victory,
And I am left to grief and pain."
Laurine replied, again: "Ah, me!
I saw the gore the lancet made!
I saw the stream from out his side!
I saw him fall, and saw him
Laid upon the leaves. He gasp'd! He died!
Oh, Death! you have your victory!"

Grew pale and woeful. From his head
Old Archus took the filigree.
In accents tremulous, he said,
"I cannot read; the heart in me
Grows heavy laden with sorrow
At the pending fate I behold
In this book of events written,
Of lovely Laurine; her lips cold
Are growing; her limbs seem smitten
With death; she says: "Yes, to-morrow!"

"What of to-morrow? Full of hope
Of expectations; of love; mirth
And joy to the world, but the scope
Of its bringing is but the birth
Of a change dreadful to Laurine;
She sinks upon the sward; her lips
Part the words: "Yes! he died for me."
Her hands falling limp as she sits
By his grave. Now I hear her say:
"To us there lies one night between."

NOTES ON LAURINE.

NOTE 1, PAGE 154. LINE 11.

"A tumulus, a man made mountain."

The mound builders have left their traces from the clear, cold lakes of the north, down through the Allegheny, Ohio, and Mississippi valleys, and on through Mexico, Central America, Peru to the Pacific ocean, leaving evidences of a population dense in numbers and of an intelligent and moral order of beings. When they lived, who they were in race development, no one knows. Their time and history are hidden in midnight darkness.

Their mounds are not only found on the American continent, but in the old world. Modern archæologists place their era long anterior to the cities of Baalbec, Palmyra and the chisled form of the Sphynx. These tumuli are very numerous in western New York, West Virginia and Ohio. The most extensive one is found on Grave creek, twelve miles below Wheeling in West Virginia. Tunneling into one, some parties found, lying in a square room, the skeletons of a man and woman. They were not Indians, but evidently of a superior race. The intellectual and moral regions were exceedingly well developed. Benevolence and reverence were large, with combativeness and destructiveness but moderately prominent. Four bracelets, made of copper, artistically designed, encircled the wrists of the corpses. The bracelets bear the appearance of having been made of copper wire, in the same manner that jewelers make them at this day. In some of the tombs were engraved copper plates, with the mastodon in harness, indicating, beyond question, that the mound-builders and the mastodon inhabited this country at the same time; and that mammoth beast had become domesticated and used in the service of man, as the horse is used by him at this day.

NOTE 2, PAGE 157, LINE 4

"Pray, good Archus, tell us how
You read these things?"

Every act done, every word spoken, every thought evolved from the brain, are for eternity and will live forever. They all make an impression, which may be read at any future time by the sensitive; on the same principle that man can call up, from the recesses of the brain, things stored there by means of that which we call memory.

Psychometry is a fact. There are persons who can take an article from a person, such as a lock of hair, handkerchief, a piece of jewelry or other thing, and by becoming passive to the interior state, read the secrets of your life, diagnose diseases and in many cases suggest proper remedies.

I have tested this power to such an extent, that I am well convinced it is possessed by some. I once made an engagement with a lady for a reading. I was instructed, when I came to see her to bring a little pebble, or other thing, and hold it in my hand, without giving it to any one, until she received it. I did so, and to my surprise, she told me where I picked up the stone, the very way I went to get to her house, and everything I did while I had it in my hand. Afterwards, while in my library, I gave her specimens of mineral from my cabinet to read, without her seeing them, which she did to my satisfaction; during the test, I had, among my selections, a large scale from an alligator, which resembled a little thin stone, or shale from a brook; when I placed it in her hand she almost went into convulsions, so great was the shock to her sensitive nerves. Through this yet unknown sense, Archus, which is an abbreviation of archæology, was able to read the life of Laurine.

JOHN DROWSY AND HIS DREAMS.

——:——

To feel the creep of gentle doze
  Enfolding thee in balmy sleep,
Becoming lost in calm repose
  As fading memory sweet
  Withdraws from its honored seat,
And leaves within itself a blank:
    Is true felicity.

To dream is when your reason sleeps
  And when your wonder ranges,
When your imagination keeps
  Your thoughts on curious changes,
  And your mind is off its hinges,
And things impossible take rank
    And guise of verity.

John Drowsy, in his lazy chair
Recumbent sat, while Betsy, fair
  As the morning, and bright
  As the jewels of night
  That deck the dorse above,
Was in her routine of duty
Of household affairs. A beauty
  She was not. Nor was love
Her chief attraction. To do her share
Was her ambition, her aim and care;
While Drowsy much preferred to dream
Than work and drudge in the routine
    Of family affairs.
    This oft engendered jars.
And made life less felicitous
Than 'twould, had it not been for this.

"Now Betsy, you just go ahead,
But let me doze," John Drowsy said—
Adjusting himself to the word,
He grew limp; and then was heard
  The gibberish of a dreaming man.
He spoke of many passing scenes:
He saw a new world in his dreams,
With many beauties, many graces.
Many grand and pleasant places
  He mentioned, as few dreamers can.

He dreamed he saw his spirit go,
He said "that he must follow too,"
He felt, he said, "as light as air"
And rising from his lazy chair
He winged his way on pinions high
Beyond the deep, blue, vaulted sky;
While neath he saw the whizzing world
Sailing onward, wheeling, twirled.
On! On it flew through boundless space,
And ever spinning in its race,
Till distance loaned to it, afar,
The diamond twinkle of a star
Set in the azure dorsy crest,
A floating orb among the rest.
Where rode the world in measured place,
Is now but found vast vacant space.
Inertia marked the silent deep,
And Quietude lay dead in sleep.
And standing in the boundless breach,
Beyond the weak, attractive reach
Of gravitation's gathering spell,
The Phasma of John Drowsy well
       Would wot a quiet rest.
Within the azure curtained sky,
His spirit cast a wistful eye
       To regions truly blest.
Away beyond his ærial sphere
Glimpsed beauties, on his vision clear.
       In a far region, new,
His awe-bewildered eye beheld
Scenes of beauty not excelled,
       In vales of tinted hue.
Crept there a soft, beatic stream,
Adown a kill enameled green,
       Beset with chrysolite.
On beds of furbished sands it ran
Through Alpine groves and mossy glen,
       In crystal wavelets bright.

On either side soft tiny grass,
    With ardent tinsels kissed the breeze,
And woodlands shed a sweet contrast,
    The heart to gladden, eye to please,
While here and there, small winding brooks,
    Through verdant dells and flowers gay,

From gushing springs to crystal lakes,
  With plaintive music wend their way.
To a clear and placid stream,
Which moves in union sweetly on,
While on its borders sportive birds
Enchant the scene with merry song.

The distance caught his furtive glance,
And bound his mind as in a trance,
  At grandeurs centered there.
Successive chains of mountains wild
Waved their ambrosial locks and smiled
    On vales of flowers fair,
    Whose fragrance filled the air
While giant trees, of living green,
Presented a transcendent scene.

Afar stretched out an ocean wide
Upon whose rolling gentle tide,
  Scudding yachts were wot to play:
And on what seemed true ether rare,
Serenely rode great ships of air,
  As grandly as ships at sea:
While, as upon a sea of glass,
A gentle folk would meet and pass
  With civic courtesies,
Indicative of training fair,
And of manners *debonair*
  For all emergencies.

John opened wide his eyes and exclaimed:
"What strange things and scenes! I be blamed
  If I don't find out
  What is hereabout.
"Where am I? Who am I? Alive?
  Or am I dead and dreaming?
  Are these scenes, so pure and seeming,
But airy ghosts, and must I strive
  To fathom the mystery
Of my being hither?
Or may I ask whether
  I may beg their history?"
While musing thus, a damsel fair
With azure eyes and auburn hair,
  Approached him with smiles
    And said:

"Dear Sir, or Madam, which you be,
It is of no concern to me,
    As sex will lose their wiles
        When dead.
This is, if you'll take my advice.
The empyrean of Paradise.

This is the land of the hereafter,
    The is to be land.
The summer land that man is after,
    The great future land.
The is to come land, where dead men go:
    Land not found in Geography,
    Described without authority
By certain dreamers, who do not know
    Of what they affirm.
    But soon you will learn
That this is the land of nowhere,
The fabled land of over there,
    The Elysian shore
    Where the saints evermore
Will sing of, but never find;
The land that lies just behind
        The grave.

The land over the river,
Which men will find never,
The land beyond the sky
To see which, you must die;
To find which your body must
Return to its mother dust.

        The grave
Must drink you in,
And you must then
Return to the original elements
From whence you came, your bones, flesh, blood,
        ligaments,
All of which compose your body
Must pass away; and nobody
        You must become,
        To make this home
The reward of an earth-spent life,
As you were not, before you had life,
When you lose life, you will again not be,

Without life where is your futurity?

Those trees with waving boughs,
  Those grand and lofty mountains,
The river that by them flows,
  Those clear and gushing fountains,
Those flowers that bloom in profusion,
  Those canons deep,
  That winding esplanade,
  That golden fruit,
  That cool inviting shade,
Are but an optical delusion.

Those things you see, you see not,
Those singing birds with wings outspread,
Those floating clouds above your head,
  That waving grass, that tiny grot,
  Yon mountain in the distance
  Have really no existence.
So is man when he gets here,
He is not here but some other where.'

"Dead!" said John, with marked chagrin,
"Have I lost the world? How? When?
  Please good angel take me back,
  Show me again my humble cot.
My hardships when upon the earth,
  Seem pleasure to me now.
I wish not a new world, new birth;
  I would return. But how?
From what I've heard, I can say,
This is not the place for me.
I'd rather be John Drowsy plain,
And be upon the earth again
With Betsy, corn bread, and hominy,
Than to be in this grand company
  A heaven born neuter.
  Oh, what a sad future!

No sex here! And this is heaven!
  Is here where all the good go?
No women. No men. Or even
  A little boy or girl. No.
All neuters here.
Neuter men. Queer.
  Neuter women.

Neuter boys and girls,
     All the same then?
How many such worlds,
I would like to know?
I'd rather stay below
     With Betsy.
How I'd like to see her!
     Poor Betsy!
     Shall I never see you more?
I know you were a little cross

And often vexed me to my sore
Discomfiture. But then I guess
     I was sometimes to blame.
     I was cross too.
     Would often do
Things, and then for the same
     Would blame you.
     Oh, Betsy! Bess!
     I would confess
My errors, could I but see you again.
Oh! The thought rives my heart with reeking pain
     And bursts my head.
     But, I am dead,
And should not feel the sadness of heart.
We were taught in life good friends must part:
     But to meet again,
     Where sorrow and pain,
     Never cross the breast
     In this region of rest.

There's one thing strange. I've often thought why
In this halcyon home in the sky,
In this beautiful land of the future
There's no men, women, girls or boys: all neuter.

                    Well,
     I'd like to know if it's so in hell?
     If it is not I will go there
     If I have to pay double fare.

What is heaven with all its joys
Without the cheer of girls and boys?
The thought of heaven would but perplex us,
Did it not have the love of the sexes.

I'd rather see the flames of hell
And risk a scorching with them,
Than even in the highest heaven dwell
Without the smiles of woman.

I'd rather face a demon mad,
With forked tongue and hisses,
Than ever be an angel clad
To feast on neuter kisses.

"Wake up, Drowsy," Betsy said
You're not in heaven, nor dead;
Not at all.
Nor are you up above the cloud,
You've been dreaming a little loud,
That is all."

SEANCE HYMN.

Oh, angels! good angels, draw near,
And let us commune with you now:
Your presence impress on us here,
And fill all our hearts with a glow.
Oh, angels! good angels, draw near,
And give us true light from above:
Dispel from our bosoms all fear,
And make them replete with your love.

Good angels, come down from above,
And cheer up poor wayfaring man;
Guide us in the sphere we should move;
Give wisdom wherever you can.
Breathe justice and mercy on all;
And drive from the bosom all strife:
Crown Amity queen of us all,
With joy in the stream of our life.

When earth shall have lost all her charms,
And we are confined here no more,
Oh, let us find rest in your arms,
To wake on the ever green shore.
Oh, angels! good angels, draw near,
And let us commune with you now:
Your presence impress on us here,
And fill every heart with a glow.

MUSIC IN THE WATERFALL.

There's strains of music soft and sweet
  Inspired everywhere,—
In rivers, lakes and oceans deep
  And in the balmy air,
There's music in the silver moon,
  And in the stars above;
There's music in the azure deep,
  And in the words of love.

CHORUS.

Oh ! there's music in the waterfall,
  Music in the trees;
Music in the childhood laugh,
  When borne upon the breeze.

There's music in the lowing herd
  As it is homeward bound;
There's music in the lambkin gay,
  When skipping o'er the ground.
There's music in the golden grain
  And in the stately tree;
There's music in the moaning wind
  And in the humming bee.
                      Chorus.

There's music in the laughing brook
  As it goes purling on;
There's music in the linnet's strain,
  And in the robin's song.
There's music in the baying hound
  When on the night wind borne:
There's music in the winding of
  The deep and mellow horn.
                      Chorus.

THERE IS NO PLACE LIKE HOME.

——:——

There is no place on earth like home
When it is true and cheerful,
But home has fled when one alone
Remains in grief and tearful.

There is no place on earth like home
When love and concord rule it,
But home has fled its sacred dome
When one, but one, can use it.

There is no place on earth like home
When converse social cheers it,
But home has lost the charms of home
When there's but one who shares it.

There is no place on earth like home
When smiles and pet words thrill it,
But home with all its sweets are flown
If there's but one to fill it.

There is no place on earth like home,
The gods, I ween, thus will it,
As well they will to make a home
There must be two to fill it.

WE ARE TO LIVE.

——:——

There is one joy, one jewel'd truth,
One fact that cheers both age and youth;
That brushes all the mists away,
And turns the night of death to day,
Disrobes the grave of all its gloom,
And glorifies the silent tomb;
That one grand truth, the spirits give,
That we first die, that we may live.

RUTH'S PLEDGE TO NAOMI.

I'll go where thou goest, and live where you live :
  Thy kindred shall be as a kindred to me;
Thy country shall take, as my country shall give :
  Thy God shall be my God; my faith is in thee:
Thy smiles will enliven my heart all anew,
  A sad thought of thine will throw gloom on my mind:
When thou will have died, I will leave all behind,
And walk to the tomb and be buried with you.

FAREWELL OLD YEAR.

Farewell old year, thy fading face
  Is ashen now with waning glories;
Thy course has been a valiant race
  And aye, will live in golden stories.

Farewell old year, with mem'ries fond,
  We scan thy life with hearts of gladness:
But see thee pass to shades profound,
  With feelings of the utmost sadness.

Farewell old year, and as we turn
  From thy receding smiles and presence,
Our hearts with raptured feelings burn
  Of mem'ries fraught with many pleasance.

Farewell old year, and we must part,
  And, ah! we know it is forever,—
You burdened with the past, depart;
  We bounding to the future, ever.

Farewell! and though it be farewell!
  Thy course is the eternal backward:
Thy space alone recalls the knell;
  Thy glories tend forever onward.

Sad are the accents of farewell,
  When tears bedew the pure shrine of love:
Sad are the thoughts that with us dwell,
  When for aye we see our friends remove.

And when we say farewell, old year,
  And close our eyes on thee forever,
Like parting friends it wrings a tear
  From out our eyes, we would not smother.

Despite those tears, our hearts enfold
  Sweet thoughts of friendships ties unbroken;
Thoughts pure of love, as burnished gold,
  Which brings us heaven as its token.

Farewell old year, but nay farewell,
  To heart-lit joys and smiling graces;
Of joys that in our bosoms dwell,
  Of kindly deeds and friendly faces.

FIFTY YEARS.

I stand upon the slant of life,
  With half a century past,
And as I ken Time's backward flow,
    I vainly try to grasp
    The fifty next to come.
The fifty that have come and gone,
  Have brought their smiles and sorrows;
Have brought their sunlight's golden beams,
    As well their storms and showers
    As they went gliding on.

As I look down those fifty years
  That I have called my own,
I see so many acts unwise,
    And so much folly done,
    I sit me down and sigh;
And yet I think I've done some good
  In those flown fifty years,
I've healed the wounds of many hearts,
    And dried up many tears
    As life went gliding by.

And something in those years have brought
  A harvest of pleasure;
And many hand-shakes dear to me—
    Many joys I treasure
    Deep in a tender heart.
Those years have found me many friends
  Whose smiles have borne me on;
Who live within the fondest thoughts
    That fruit the rushing throng
    Of years as they depart.

Oh, yes! Those fifty fleeting years
  Have been a school to me—
Have been so many teachers true,
  That now I plainly see
What Time has helped me learn—
And Time is a teacher trite and true
  That will withstand the test—
It taught me this: Of treasures won,
  That smiles will pay the best
And bring the best return.

May 26, 1884.

TWENTY YEARS OF VICE.*

Aristo was an artist, and so deft was he, as such,
That nature seemd to smile anew at his most skilful touch;
Yet, with his skill in paints, he wore a heavy hanging eye,
Portraying that his heart suppressed a deep and hidden sigh.

To drive the mien of gloom away, that wrestled with his soul,
He sought, within a busy mart, to take an idle stroll;
When, gazing through the broad highway, his eyes, with
    gleam of joy,
Fell on a most angelic form, a blooming little boy.

The lad so charm'd his swelling heart, that he forgot his woe,
And felt he had a world of bliss within his studio,
If he could get a sitting from the boy, so fair and gay,
That sported such a comely face, so innocent at play.

"My little man, I would delight to paint your picture free,
If you will stop your play awhile, and take a walk with me,
To where my studio is found, a neat and cosy place,
Where I can rightly use my brush, to paint your pretty face."

Hand in hand they walked along, the child as if on duty,
Not dreaming that he was, himself, the empire of beauty;
The child beheld so many things, in the room, beguiling,
But most surprised when he saw himself on canvas smiling.

So perfect was this child of bliss, upon the canvas born,
The artist placed it where his eyes could see it night and
    morn;
And when his spirits drooped, in gloom, he sought this pic-
    ture fair,
Whose face of innocence, sublime, dispelled all gloom and
    care.

Years came and went, and in their course, brought riches
and renown
To the artist, who was inspired to keep all feelings down,
That would conduce to thoughts impure by looking at the
face
Of this fair child of innocence, which did his heart enchase.
He wondered, often, what had become of that once hand-
some boy,
Whether he had grown up to shame, or to his friends a joy.
One day, while walking down the street, he saw a man forlorn,
Whose mien was so forbidding that the dogs passed by in
scorn.
The artist thought the subject was so lorn in the extreme,
He'd take him to his studio and sketch a beggar scene.
The pose was through—the artist saw, the child, the beggar
eyeing,
Then turned he from the picture, with his eyes suffused
with crying.
"Oh ! chide me not, old artist now," the beggar said, and
sobbed,
"The smile that parts that glowing face, long years ago, I
robb'd—
"Twas twenty years ago when I came here, at your advice.
A smiling child, now here again, with twenty years of vice."

*The idea was taken from a story in a Catholic Reader.

THE GODS.

Men think, labor, scheme, contend,
　　Pray, sing and fight for gods unknown;
When all is o'er, their achievements end,
　　In dreamless silence in the tomb.

Whose tongueless eloquence appeal
　　In solemn accents low, sublime,
For man to guard his highest weal
　　And surcease war for gods divine.

For gods and ghosts and sprites unseen,
　　Are but the myths of shadows shed,
And when you die for them, I ween,
　　You'll find that they like you are dead.

Gods come and go, and pass away,
　　As seen by mouldering temples thick,
And those whose fanes are seen to-day,
　　Are either dead or very sick.

LIFE.

—— : ——

All life is one unfathomed span—
A constant flow, through matter borne
With no Causation's moving plan
  Superior to crude matter shown.

Forms and expressions come and go;
' Worlds form, dissolve and pass away,
But life is ever in its flow;
  It knows no birth and no decay.

Life is the only thing that lives,
  Its flow is its eternal noon;
It spans the two eternities,
  While rev'ling in its morning bloom.

Time, matter, space, the trinity
  Whose presence boundless force traverse,
Which form'd that patent unity,
  The vast, the formless universe.

When Time, in its infinitude,
  Shall wear an old and furrowed brow,
Life will through all its certitude,
  Have but one throbbing, pregnant now.

Life knows no past, no future own,
  The present is its only meed:
No time but now was ever known,
  The now will ever now succeed.

The past, with all its its fruits has flown,
  The future has not yet arrived,
The pregnant now is all we own,
  It is the all of either side.

Life like Pegasus flying on
  From place to place, from town to town,
Well freighted with a human throng
  Of existence. On, ever on.

With even pace this life-fraught car
  Bears all along to one grand goal,
On through a flight that leads afar,
  The longing of the human soul.

It recks not where, but speeds away,
  On th' wings of Time not to return—

It bears all to one destiny,
One pending fate, one common bourne.

No special car moves in this train,
No seats reserved for sect, or clan,
Here all are on one level plain,
All travel here as fellowman.

YOSEMITE.

Word pictures must fail, when the Yosemite speaks,
Its huge colonades and high-reaching peaks,
Its grandeur and beauty of feature sublime,
Send echoing back the chaste rhythms of time.

Frill'd with great carvings, on its adamant face,
Whose wrinkles and fissures Time only can trace,
All cleft from rock mountains, by waters entwirl'd,
The acme of beauty and awe of the world.

The waters come down with a plunge and a leap,
From rifts in the sky, to a gnarl'd yawning deep,
A huge granite basin, where it writhes and boils,
Girates and contorts, like a demon in toils.

Drunk on the charms of the amethyst there,
Infusing its hue in the diamond-decked air,
Whose face is surcharged with a crysolite trail,
Enwoofed with the gauze of an aqueous veil.

Hung up and let down with a capricious will,
An artist would wist, by the tints of the kill,
So deftly arranged, with blendings so rare,
That the limner of heav'n had his studio there.

Deep drapery the face of the pyramid shrouds,
Festoon'd and entwin'd to the *Rest of the Clouds*;
Pearl wreathed and inlac'd with silver tipp'd spray,
Bedighted with diamonds, in matchless display.

Old Cathedral grand, in deep gloom towers there,
Where Silence at vespers retires for prayer;
And awe fills the breast, at manifold pages,
Of Nature revealed, through this book of ages.

Cholock is famed for its broken up mountains,
Its wilder cascades and arrow jet fountains,

Its cataracts mad and its carved gorges deep,
That dash down the streamlets, from steep upon steep.

Stand there, the rock walls, three thousand feet high,
And domes, steep, upreaching, which dazzle the eye:
Where Canopah sits, with an adamant will,
And Tusayac breaks the smooth glide of the kill.

There Merced tumbles down, with a dash and a roar,
Then wends its way off, through a fern cover'd floor,
And purls as it goes.   As the Awanee leaps,
For the tongue to be still, while Yosemite speaks.

RELIGIOUS WARS.

If a tower was built, for each one that had sank, (1)
   In death from the cause of religion;
There would not be room, on the valley or bank,
   To give them a place for erection.

If the veins that have bled, since the crusades began,
   Were permitted to flow in one stream,
There would be such a flood at thy instance, Oh, man!
   That the world hath not heretofore seen.

If the groans of the dying, were blended in one,
   It would make such a dolorous sound,
That all space would be shook, from the earth to the sun,
   Like an earthquake convulsing the ground.

If all of the treasures, inhumanely spent,
   Had been placed to relieve the distress'd,
The world would to-day, wear a smile of content,
   And feel that god's blessings had bless'd.

But the record of blood, shed in Palestine old,
   Is a record that shocks our senses;   ·
The records, the tenth of which never was told
   And never return'd recompenses.

The stories are those of black carnage and crime:
   To capture a long vacated tomb;
Where crimes were forgiven in advance of the time,
   To illumine fair heaven with gloom.

Those crimes are embellish'd in history and song,
   Farther back than at Joshua's fight;

When the moon stood still, o'er the vale Ajalon,
And the sun over Gibeon's site.

Those wars have drap'd all the ages in shame,
And smote with a blightening rod,
The face of the land with both rapine and flame,
For the glory of one common god. (2)

At the wage of each battle the caliph would pray
God that success, his arms might betide;
The pope to the same Aba Father would say:
"Help us slaughter the vile other side."

Thus for years, one hundred and seventy-seven, (3)
Both sides, for aid, to the same god appeal'd;
Both slaughtered to people, alike, the same heaven,—
And fought for the same bible reveal'd.

NOTE I.

"What is that? Town of Ramleh, birthplace, residence and the tomb
of Samuel, the glorious prophet. Near by tower of forty martyrs, called because that number of disciples perished there for Christ's sake; but if towers
had been built for all those who in the time of wars as in the time of peace
have fallen on this road during the ages past, you might almost walk on tur-
rets from Joppa to Jerusalem." —DeWitt Tamage, in his sermon on the Land
of Palestine, Oct. 6th, 1890.

NOTE 2.

"For the glory of one common god."
The Mohammedans, like the Christians, take the bible as the root of their
religion. They both believe in the Jehovah of the Jews and in the New testament, but differ as to the Koran. The Koran teaches that "God is God
and Mohammed is his prophet. This pretense the Christians deny, hence their
mutual hatred and slaughter.

NOTE 3.

"Thus for years, one hundred and seventy-seven."
The Caliph Omar having taken Jerusalem, A. D. 637. the places held
most sacred to the christians passed to the control of the Mussulmen. The
christians were allowed, by paying a small tax, to visit the city of Jerusalem,
the holy sepulchre and the church of the resurrection.
In the 10th century, the Fatimite Caliphs, under their control of affairs,
the christians were maltreated. Their pilgrimages were interfered with, and
many of the holy places were defaced. These outrages greatly excited the
christians of Europe, who were at a very low standard of enlightenment at
the time, and a crusade was inaugurated by Peter the Hermit and started for
the Holy Land in the spring 1096. There were eight crusades in all; the
last one ending with the defeat of the army of Prince Edward of England in
the year 1271. Thus leaving Jerusalem still in the hands of the Turks, where
it is to-day.

SAVE YOUR GOLD.

—:—

Let go of gold! Let go of gold!
  I hear it sung by young and old;
  I hear it from the pulpit cold.
Let go of gold! Let go of gold!

The beggar mouths it in the streets.
Then asks for alms from all he meets:
The spendthrift sows it wide and far,
As though it is unworth a care:
The crank, whose fam'ly is in want,
Knows how to run the government:
And from his foolish lips we're told
The rich should share with him their gold.

But when they have grown gray and old,
With not a shelter from the cold:
They then regret the end foretold,
Of those who sacrifice their gold.

If you have doubts, what you should do,
Ask of the child without a shoe:
Ask of the mother's tearful eyes:
Ask of the infant's starving cries:
Ask of the toiler, day by day,
Who works and groans on scanty pay:
Ask of the girls who run the loom:
Ask of the man, whose heart of gloom,
Can know not how the crust of bread
Can feed the mouths that must be fed:
Ask of the old man, what to save,
As he goes, ragged, to the grave:
They all will say, in accents bold,
To work, while young, and save your gold.

'TIS FOUR O'CLOCK.

—:—

[Reply to "Lines" written on the anniversary of a marriage.]

TO H.

'Tis four o'clock, the brazen bell
  Rings out upon the fretful air,
And by its golden intones tell
  When thee, my dear, strong, hale and fair
Became my wife, five years ago.

'Tis four o'clock, and well my mind,
  A record of thy beaming eyes
And precious self keeps, when we timed
  The hour and the nuptial ties
Made thee my wife, five years ago.

'Tis four o'clock, with heart on fire,
  Still with love; would that we invade
That shrine again that will inspire
  Our hearts so true, when we were made
Husband and wife, five years ago.

'Tis four o'clock, five years have passed.
  Thy cheeks are wan, thy health hath flown,
And yet it is my heaven's task
  To love thee more than I dared own.
When made my wife, five years ago.

'Tis four o'clock, short seems the time,
  When hand in hand and heart in heart,
I vowing thine, thou vowing mine.
  And we assumed that hallowed part—
Husband and wife, five years ago.

'Tis four o'clock, a joyous hour,
  When my heart plim'd with love for thee
And thine became the plighted power
  To bless me through eternity;
My little wife, five years ago.

December 31, 1890.

THE SUNNY SOUTH.

The sunny south! the sunny south! the glory of the day:
The meed of true devotion, the grandest in display.
Where men of nerve are born, to wield the power great and
    grand;
Where ladies wear the graces of a proud and favor'd land;
Where liberty is cradled in the heart of every one,
And valor, as an heirloom, sent from father to each son.

The sunny south! the sunny south! thy fame shall still arise.
The pride of every valiant son, where love of country lies:
The field of many battle scars, where valor was defied,
Where sank in death contending foes, that sleep now, side
    by side:

Who claim alike a tear of grief, that war of sorrow wrung;
Who bare their breasts a targe to each, but sank in death
    as one.
The sunny south! the sunny south! while ages come and go,
Thy sons will wear the pride of men, 'mid friends or chaff-
    ing foe;
With nerves of steel and loyal aim, thine is their common cause,
Thy meed is what they most esteem, with rules of right,
    and laws,
That bear alike on all concerned, be they the weak or strong,
That all may feel a fitting pride in one great gonfalon.

A TEMPERANCE OATH.

         I swear!
By all the unwept, marshal'd dead,
By all the hearts that rum has bled,
By all the wealth that vice consumes,
By all who die of whisky fumes,
By all the paupers in the land,
By all the days we have been damn'd.
By all the man-destroying gnomes,
By all the scattered, bleaching bones,
Which have, for ages past, been strown,
Before the gate of manhood's throne;
By all the crimes, by all the deeds,
By all the dens that whisky feeds;
By all the orphans and their cries,
By all the woe beneath the skies;
By all the guilt, where misery reigns,
By all the blood that drench the plains:
Besmear the hills, enrich the vales.
By all the anguish crime entails;
By all the demons chained in hell,
By all the loathsome things that dwell
Beneath the eye of guilt and shame,
By all the devils, by the name
Of all the imps that should be damn'd,
And stricken from this rum-curs'd land.
         I swear!
That I will strive, do all I can,
To kill this common foe of man,
And hurl him from his lofty state,
To feel its sting—a felon's fate.

ANTIETAM.

——:——

As long as courage has a place
Within the heart, the human race,
Admire will, the dauntless men
Who battled at Antietam.

Both armies knew their chieftains well,
And both surg'd in the battle fell;
Rang out the din of war on high;
Dense clouds of smoke begrim'd the sky.
Death! grim and anger'd vied to reign;
And leap'd the hot and angry flame;
As rang the cannon's sullen sound
That arch'd the heavens; shook the ground.
All through the valleys, hills and plain,
The wound with the nerveless slain
Gave evidence, that shot and shell,
Were doing but their work too well.
And still the rush and steady tread,
Reck'd not the storm of raining lead,
But in the face of foemen strong,
Each foeman pressed the battle on.
'Mid routs and shouts of victory,
The dust and smoke enwrapp'd the sky
In sable folds, grim streaked with red
By shooting flames that illum'd the bed
Where Carnage blew his stifling breath
And foes, companion'd, lay in death.

There rife and terror seemed to reign,
The missiles flew and leaped the flame,
Yet foemen, dauntless moved ahead,
Amid the storm of raining lead.
Hand to hand to death contended,
In maddened streams their blood was blended,
And many sank without a groan,
But yet the maddened storm went on.
Daunting not at danger rife,
Weighing not the chance of life;
Charges received and charges made,
Where dead and dying soldiers laid
In heaps, there lying course by course,
As winnowed in a ghastly corse.
A yell, a shout,—redoubled charge,

As thousands bore their breasts a targe.
A volley rang along the plain,
And fell a thousand warriors slain;
A thousand warriors bowed the head;
A thousand numbered with the dead;
Depleted ranks they heeded not.
Surged the living and still they fought,
Beneath the waving stars and bars,
And others fought beneath the stars,
There, proudly waving overhead,
Shedding luster on the dead,
Who died as Union soldiers brave,
That still their country's flag might wave:
To kiss the breeze so gallantly,
That fans the land of liberty.
Exhausted both the armies then,
And peace arose on Antietam.

CONTENTS.